LUCELLE;

OR,

THE YOUNG INDIAN.

—————

A ROMANCE.

—————

LONDON :

PUBLISHED BY E. LLOYD, 12, SALISBURY-SQUARE,
FLEET-STREET.

LUCELLE;

OR,

THE YOUNG INDIAN.

INTRODUCTION

OUR object in publishing a novel of so much interest, will, we doubt not, be duly appreciated by our very numerous and intellectual readers. At times, when we could not introduce history, we have endeavoured to place, in its stead, the interesting objects of fiction, founded upon facts. In the present instance, that thrilling and truly interesting subject, "Love," is the meteor of our present occupation.

No. 1.

We beg very respectfully to introduce to our readers the novel of "Lucelle; or, the Young Indian," under the very *positive* impression of their reading.

———

CHAPTER I.

THE world may laugh, and sneer and jeer as much as it pleases, and pretend to look upon love as a " very little thing," but after all, so long as the human heart is constituted as it is, this passion will continue to be like the rod of the ancient prophet, the master feeling of the soul. No dramatic composition is bearable unless it is well spiced with the " tender passion," and a work of fiction would be as dry as a last year's robin's nest, unless those peculiar emotions which draw the two sexes together have a very conspicuous place in it, and form one of the leading features of the story.

Men and women, collectively, may affect to despise a drama, or a novel which contains a large quantity of love sick stuff, when talking about such compositions ; but, individually, they are governed by this very thing which they affect to ridicule and laugh at so much. They have two characters, an exterior and an interior, and it may be difficult for even intimate friends or familiar acquaintances to determine which predominates. Every one knows his own heart and his private history, except so far as his sins may be concerned ; to these he may be, and probably is blind. But few of the human race have ever lived to the age of puberty, who have not, at some period of their lives, fallen in love, as the phrase goes. That is an epoch in human life which youth most vividly remembers, and age cannot erase it from the tablets of the heart. In six of the seven ages which the Bard of Avon has so graphically described, the passion of love is strongly felt, or the time distinctly remembered when it first threw its halo about the heart. So strong does this sentiment reign in the human breast, that when one object of affection is lost, the heart puts forth its feelers for another to fill the aching void, even before the time has expired during which common decency, habit, or custom has decreed that outward signs of mourning should be worn. No class so soon falls in love as widows and widowers. Even the youth whose heart sighs like a furnace, feels not the tenderness which beauty and loveliness inspire sooner than those of riper years, who have lost the objects of their first attachment ; and we have no reason to doubt but the lean and slippered pantaloon, whose hose are a world too wide for his shrunk shanks, has still the emotions of love. We have never known a widow, however much the infirmities of age might bend her down, who did not cherish a wish, and sometimes indulge a secret hope, that she should be married again ; or, if he was a bachelor, that he expected every day that some circumstance would happen which would introduce him to some fair woman. How often men wish, and even hope for certain things, without lifting a finger to obtain them! Well, hope keeps the heart from breaking, and makes life tolerable.

When Queen Elizabeth requested Shakspeare to write a play, and introduce into it his unimitated and inimitable Falstaff as a lover, she only reflected the spirit of the age in which she lived. Although never married herself yet she thought as much about love as any of her loving subjects. She might have been too proud to marry, but she was not too cold to love. The queen, when she gave this order to the great poet, not only made known her own feelings and represented the feelings of her subjects, but also embodied those emotions which have actuated the human heart in every age of the world. The people of all nations who have cultivated and cherished a fondness for dramatic literature poetry, music, and works of fiction, have always been more excited by love passages than by any other single idea advanced in such productions. The Chinese may be an exception; for it is said that filial love takes a more prominent place in their novels than any other passion or affection of the soul. Why the people of the Celestial Empire should form an exception to the general rule, and esteem filial love more than any other sentiment of the heart, is more than we can tell. This quality of the Chinese heart, must be attended with very happy consequences, and necessarily makes very obedient and loving children. If such a sentiment could be more generally diffused through the world, it would unquestionably render family government a much more easy task than it is now. But we will not stop to discuss any grave questions of philosophy or metaphysics, for such subjects more properly belong to other pages than to these.

It was in the summer of 1759 when our story commences. The Colonial and Indian wars had been very bloody, and were not yet terminated. The advantages which the English had obtained over the French in several campaigns encouraged the British Minister to hope that the conquest of Canada was near at hand. Three expeditions were therefore projected: one against Quebec, under the command of General Wolfe, one against the forts on Lake Champlain, under General Amherst, who was commander-in-chief of the British forces in America, and one against the French fort at Niagara, to be conducted by General Prideux, and Sir William Johnson. The conquest of Quebec was regarded as the most important, and the most difficult object of the campaign. On the shore of Lake Champlain, within a cannon shot of Ticonderoga, lived an old Frenchman by the name of De la Motte. He had resided in this place many years, but had never interested himself in the wars which had been raging in the Canadas, and among Colonists and Indians. Several years previous to the commencement of our story, he had buried a wife and two children; but he had one left, a daughter, by the name of Lucelle, a most beautiful female, bright and musical as the lark, and active and sprightly as the deer of her own native forest. She was now about eighteen years of age, and the first-born of the old Frenchman's family. As might be reasonably expected, she was the idol of her father and pet of all who knew her; but the circle of her acquaintances and friends was very limited. The profession of her father was hunting, and he cared for nothing else. M. de la Motte had always secured the friendship of the Indians, and maintained a perfectly neutral position among the belligerent parties.

His lodge was within a stone's throw of the lake, situated on the south side of a high bluff, which extended quite down to the lake's shore, and protected the hut of the hunter from the cold north winds during the inclement seasons of the year. A small brook trickled by his habitation and mingled its waters with those of the lake, forming a little harbour for his birch canoe, which Lucelle delighted to skim over the lake during the summer season. She never felt better than when she was paddling the canoe over the calm bosom of the lake with a paddle ingeniously wrought by her own hands. The vessel was made by a young Iroquois Indian, and purchased of him by her father. This son of the forest had often seen Lucelle and would have loved her if he had dared to do so. At any rate, the canoe was more beautifully made and nicely finished because the young Iroquois knew that the fair Lucelle would sometimes sail in it as well as her father.

We may as well describe the person of our herione now as at any other time. Her form was light, but yet every muscle had full play when she moved, giving her a graceful fulness and beauty of motion which might have become the most fashionable saloons of Paris better than the humble sequestered dwelling she occupied. Her complexion was a beautiful brunette, her hair black as the raven's wing, and fell in rich clusters over her finely moulded neck and shoulders her eyes were very dark and sparkled with great brilliancy when she was excited but in her calmer moments their sparkling brilliancy did not destroy that softness of expression which love is calculated to produce in prince or peasant, her forehead was not high and broad, neither was it low nor pinched up at the temples, but it was expanded just enough to give the beholder a correct idea of beauty, and at the same time it impressed him with the assurance, that there was no lack of intellectual power in the fair possessor, her nose was beautifully chisselled, and the expression about her mouth evinced great firmness and resolution, as well as mirth and quick wit.   On the whole, her face and form were exceedingly beautiful and bewitching.   No young man of taste and refinement could see her and remain an indifferent spectator.   The French officers and soldiers, who at that time occupied the fort of Ticonderoga, were all smitten with her charms, but she had invariably pursued such a course of conduct, whenever she happened to meet them, that they dared not make any advances beyond what strict modesty and true delicacy would approve and justify.

Although she appeared by her conduct and motions to be entirely ingorant of her charms, and her powers to please the other sex, yet she was not so.   Many a time had she looked into the mirrored surface of the lake, while she was dexterously paddling her canoe over it, and beheld her beautiful face and curling hair reflected from the deep bosom of the waters.   Ah! she had all the instincts of an accomplished woman in civilized and polished life.   These taught her that she was beautiful and possessed powers to please.   And often had she said within herself that she could exercise them whenever an object was presented which she deemed worthy of her heart.   Strange as it may seem, Lucelle was ambitious, and determined to seek fame and reputation in some way.   The spirit and enthusiasm of the times inspired her young heart with strange fancies, and excited within her bosom emotions of ambition.   She could not, like her father, remain neutral and indifferent to the scenes which surrounded them.   They lived in the midst of wars most cruel and blood-thirsty.   While her father cared not which government he lived under, whether of France or England, her feelings and impulses were all on the side of the former.   She disliked the British, and yet she sometimes dreamed of having a British officer of high rank and wealth for her husband, in case she could not obtain a French one.

One morning, in the latter part of July, she was off upon the lake in her canoe.   The weather was very fine.   Scarcely a single cloud as big as her fair hand could be seen any where above the horizon.   It was towards noon, and not a breath of air rippled the calm surface of the lake.   The sunbeams lay upon the placid waters and made them shine like burnished silver.   The trees upon the shore were deeply laden with green foliage, and the high bluff around Tinconderoga looked beautiful and grand.   Mansfield Mountain and Camel's Hump raised their lofty summits far above the clouds on the eastern side of the lake, and range after range of mountains rose one after another upon the western shore of this beautiful sheet of water, the whole forming one of the grandest and most picturesque views to be seen in any country.   Lucelle was letting her boat lay calm and still upon the water, and admiring the beautiful scenery which surrounded her.   She sometimes wished that she could be the mistress of some splendid establishment, and then again it would seem hard for her to leave the lodge where she was born and the little trout brook which trickled along by its side. A thousand ambitious emotions pressed her heart, and a thousand fancies flitted across her mind.   She thought of the wars, and even of seeking the bubble reputation at the cannon's mouth.

"Oh ! how I should like to be engaged in a battle!" she said to herself as she sat in her light canoe, looking towards the fort, and saw French soldiers promenading upon the steep bluff which rises perpendicularly up from the shore of the lake, and prevents all approach from that quarter. "But it is not so pleasant to be fired at, or cut in pieces by a British sword. The young Indian told me the other day that it was expected the British soldiers would attack the fort in the course of the summer. My father has two guns, and one of them is just big enough for me. I have shot a good many ducks and other game with it, and why couldn't I shoot a British officer with it? Ah! I had better shoot him with my bright eyes, and make a husband of him. Father says he don't care who beats, if the otters and beavers are not frightened off by their guns. Strange he don't take sides with the French, his own nation; I don't so much wonder that he don't fight for the British. They've always been the enemies of the French, and trying to make slaves of them. He says, if they will let him alone and permit him to roam the fields, he will not disturb them. Hunting has great charms for him I like the sport of the chase too, but then there are some other things I love better : at any rate, I think I should love them better"

These and many other things ran through the mind of the lovely and ambitious Lucelle as she sat in her boat, viewing the beautiful prospect around her.

"It is a lovely day," she continued to muse to herself. "But it is really warm. No cool breeze from the north has yet sprung up to ripple the smooth surface of the lake, and the reflection of the sun from the water is quite oppressive. I think I must leave this beautiful spot and seek the shade."

While she thus communed with her own thoughts, she cast her eyes towards the shore, and saw the young Iroquois sitting on a rock at the mouth of the brook, where she moored her light canoe, and gazing upon her. This young fellow was one of the handsomest Indians belonging to any of the numerous tribes which were then scattered over the country. He was about twenty two years of age, tall and straight as an arrow, of quick and easy motions, and courage which knew no danger. As we have before intimated, he would have loved Lucelle, if he had dared to be so presumptuous; but he never breathed such a thought to her. His acts and every motion evinced he was her faithful friend, if not her lover. She had never yet seen any white man she esteemed so highly as she did him, but she did not love him. Such a thought as that never found a lodgment in her mind. She was too proud and aspiring to marry a red son of the forest, and her heart was too kind not to return the friendship he had manifested towards her. They were indeed friends, and not unfrequently seen together on the shores of the lake, with their guns, but sometimes in the forest, two or three hours' walk from her father's lodge, insomuch that the officers and soldiers of the fort began to speak of them as lovers. She was aware of this; but then she had too much independence of mind and character to be annoyed by it.

When she saw this Iroquois at the landing place of her boat, she gracefully plied her paddle, and her light vessel swept over the water like a duck, and soon its neatly curved nose was run into the brook. She leaped upon the rock where he sat, and bid him a cordial good morning.

"Where have you been these two or three days?" she inquired. "I haven't seen you since last Monday. Have you been hunting, or looking after the British ?"

"I have been up the lake," he replied. "I saw some of my red brethren about thirty miles south from here, and they told me Gen. Amherst would oe here one of these days with an army, and make an attack upon the fort."

"Do you think he will come?" asked Lucelle, gazing upon his copper-coloured face, as if she would read his thoughts before his tongue expressed them.

"I don't know what to think," he replied. "The British feel now quite encouraged, and intend to drive the French from the country or make slaves of them. I shouldn't be surprised if an attempt was made to take the fort before many weeks. The British are rallying their forces at many points. It is said they intend to attack Quebec too."

"Ah!" they cannot conquer that strong place," she said. "I went there last summer with my father, the longest journey I ever made. But we went by water almost all the way. I used to paddle our canoe a good deal of the way myself. We had a good many furs, and father brought home quite a pile of silver and gold with him."

"What does he expect to do with all his money?" inquired the young Indian, while a smile passed over his countenance, and he gazed on the beautiful countenance of the fair Lucelle.

"That's more than I can tell you," she replied. "He loves to hoard it up to look at it. He has been accumulating it ever since I was born. He sometimes, in the evening, takes it out from the boxes and counts it all over, and then carefully puts it away again."

"He's laying it up for you," he replied. "You'll have a good fortune left when he dies."

".I don't care anything about money, unless I should have enough of it to buy the best house in Quebec, and live there," she answered. "And then, if the British should conquer it, I shouldn't care about living there."

"If you could marry a rich officer, and live in a splendid house, you would like, I conclude," he replied. "Oh, Lucelle, you're proud and ambitious. I would not leave these woods, where I have always lived, for all the splendour in the world. I love the brooks, the lakes, the mountains, and the valleys. All have charms for me."

"I love all these things too, but then there are other fine things in the world I should like to see," she replied. "I should like to live in London or Paris. I've often heard father speak of those cities. You say I'm proud. Well, I know I am, and how can I help it? It is born in me, and will show itself."

"I expect you will be some great lady yet, and I hope you will be, if you wish to be," he answered. "You are a white woman, and such are sometimes very proud ; but I'm an Indian, and never can be great, however much I desire it. I sometimes wish I was white, but then it is wrong to indulge such wishes."

"You must marry some Indian girl as handsome as yourself, and then you will be just as happy as if you were white, and a great man," she answered. "I often think if I were less ambitious I should be more happy ; but still I sigh for something beyond what this beautiful forest affords. I sometimes think I will take up arms, disguise myself as a young man, and fight the English. I don't see why I couldn't shoot them as well as I can shoot wild ducks. I've often beat father down in yonder cove, and killed more at a shot than he ever did. He says I would make a noble soldier, but he wouldn't let me take up arms on either side. He thinks of nothing but beavers, otters, or anything which will bring him in the money. I have asked him many times why he was so anxious for silver and gold ; but he always put me off, and said he would tell me one of these days."

"Perhaps he means to go back to France again," said her friend.

"Never, I think, so long as otters swim and beavers build their dams," she replied.

"Then why does he want money?' he inquired. "Surely a white man can't be such a fool as to work so hard to lay up money merely to look at. Why not go down to the shore of the lake and pick up some smooth stones and lay them up to look at ?"

"Oh, white folks are sometimes misers, and I've often thought my father was one," she replied. "Men love money for it's own sake, and not for the good it may bring them."

The young Iroquois had no proper conception of what a miser is, and could have no idea what a man should want money for, unless he bought something with it. To love money as he did his wampum was a mystery to him. He thought it looked well enough, but its beauty alone, aside from any use, was not inducement enough for him to toil so hard for it as M. de la Motte did.

"I cannot understand you, or if I do, it seems to me you misjudge your father's motives," he replied. "He does not work so hard to lay up gold and silver, for the sake of gratifying his eyes with the sight of it. No, no, Lucelle. Your father has some motive beyond all this. I think I once heard him say he should like to go to Paris before he dies, if he could go as he would like to."

"Did you hear him say that?" she anxiously inquired, feeling as if she should be much gratified to live in that great city.

"I'm quite sure I did hear him speak such a wish, but he did not say he should go," he replied.

"Oh! I wish he would go," said Lucelle, much overjoyed at the thought, believing she would there realise some of her dreams of splendour and high life.

"What! and leave all these beautiful scenes which have afforded you so much pleasure ever since you were born," he said in a sorrowful tone of voice. "What would you do with the canoe I made for you, when you leave? You would not need it there, for you couldn't carry this lake with you, and there may be no water there over which you could paddle it as you have here to-day. Ah! you would sigh for your native forests agan, and wish yourself once more in your canoe on the lake whose waters have borne you up so many years."

"Oh, I would give you the canoe to remember me by," she replied smiling.

"I should not need such a gift to make me remember you," he replied, looking at the sparkling waters of the brook as they ran into the lake, and not daring to gaze into her dark eyes lest he should betray the tender emotions which swelled his bosom.

"You might remember me for a few weeks after I was gone, without the boat," she replied. "But if I should give it you, it would remind you of me so long as it should last.

"And think you I should forget you after the canoe was gone?" he inquired, "Ah! I fear me you don't know an Indian's heart. When he once likes, he never forgets, and if he hates, it is the same."

"Then may Heaven forbid that you should ever hate me," she replied. "It would grieve me most bitterly to know that my best friend, next to my father, had turned against me."

"Then you believe that I am your friend," he said, while a crimson blush might have been seen under his copper skin.

"Do you ask me such a question?" she inquired, feeling somewhat surprised that he should institute such an inquiry, and with such apparent seriousness, "Yes, I not only believe, but I think I know you are my friend and the friend of my good father. All the Indians are his friends: for he has treated them with kindness. However much the different tribes may be enemies to each other, they have all been his friends."

"Your father is a very cunning man," he replied. "He not only knows how to trap otter or beaver, but also how to please Indians. He never steals their fur, and therefore they will not steal his. Indians know when a white man uses them well, and they will return the favour. Give an Indian meat when he is hungry and he never forgets it, and besides all that, he will tell all the other Indians of it. Your father once gave my father food on a cold winter's day, when he was almost starved, and I heard him tell many Indians of it. I was a little boy then, but I have remembered it ever since. My father died soon after that, for he was then old."

"I never heard my father speak of it," she replied, feeling a gratification to know that her father had been kind to her friend's father.

"Perhaps not," he answered. "It was not long after you were born. He has given so many Indians food that he may have forgotten this deed of charity."

"I will ask him," said Lucelle, "I didn't know that he was acquainted with your father. I'm glad he was.

"O, yes, he was well acquainted with him," he replied. "They once found a beaver's dam together, and set their traps for them, but your father was the most lucky, for his traps caught five out of the seven, I heard my father tell of that too, but the world could'nt have made him believe that your father took any of the five from his traps, and cheated him. No, no, he was lucky, and knew as well as Indians how to set his traps."

"No he would not cheat Indians or any one else," she replied, turning her head round as she spoke, and her eyes fell on a French officer belonging to the fort, whose name was Delano, a lieutenant in the service. He was standing upon an elevated spot within gunshot of them, and gazing very intently. Lucelle started when she saw him, but did not let the young officer know that she discovered him. She knew him perfectly well, for he had followed her round in several places before, and had been twice at her father's lodge. Her opinion of him was not very favourable to his honour or integrity. She had seen enough to satisfy her that he sought her society for no honourable purposes, and she had always avoided him. The young Indian also saw him. and was not well pleased with seeing him thus standing and gazing upon them. After a few more words had passed between them, Lucelle went into the lodge, and her friend struck off into the woods

---

CHAPTER II.

WHEN Lucelle entered the lodge, her father was reclining upon a rudely constructed bench partially asleep, but he awoke from his slumber, when he heard the light footfalls of his daughter. He saw at a glance that she was somewhat excited.

"Where have you been, Lucelle, since you came ashore?" inqnired her father, rising up and lighting his pipe. "I thought I saw you paddling towards the landng some time ago."

"I was," she replied. "When I ran the canoe up into the brook, I saw young Turok there and stopped to converse with him. He told me that you once gave his father food when he was almost famished with hunger, and he never forgot it."

"I did, Lucelle," he replied. "But how could he know? He was but a little boy then."

"Oh, he said his father told him of it," she answered. "But he thought that you might not remember the circumstance, because you had given so many Indians food."

"Ah! Lucelle, I remember it well," he replied, while a smile lit up his wrinkled and weather-beaten countenance. "It happened on a day which I never shall forget ?"

"Why not forget that day as well as any other?" she inquired, feeling her curiosity much excited, and being anxious to hear the reason.

"It was the day when you were born," he replied. "That was seventeen years ago last January, and so you're very near eighteen, an age when young women begin to think about b. ing married.

"I hav'nt thought much about that yet, father," she replied. " I hav'nt seen any one yet I should be willing to have."

"I hope not," he said. "Time enough yet these dozen years for you."

"But do tell me about young Turok's father," she said. "I want to hear more about him."

"Don't you prefer to hear something about his son !" said the old man, smiling and gazing very quaintly into Lucelle's face.

"I have seen him, but I have seen his father," she replied. "You do not think, father, that I particularly love the young Indian, do you ? He's our friend, and as such I respect and highly esteem him.—He's one of the handsomest Indians I have ever seen, and he's good too, as he is handsome, but I never would marry an Indian, if he was made of gold."

"Well, well, Lucelle, I was only joking," he replied. "I did not suppose you would. Turok is a nice fellow, and his father was a very clever man. When he was quite old, he came here in a dreadful storm in the month of January. It happened to be the very day you came among us. He had been several days out and a storm coming on, he could neither reach his own wigwam as soon as he calculated, nor kill any game for food. When he came in, he was almost ex-

hausted with hunger and fatigue. I gave him a little food along by degrees, and he recovered so much that the next day he was able to proceed on to his camp, which was then about ten miles from here. I never saw any human being manifest so much gratitude as that poor old Indian did. He had a powerful frame, and a robust constitution, but to be almost three days without food came very near costing him his life. If he had had five miles farther to travel through

No. 2.

the deep snow that day, he would never have reached my shelter. His little dog came almost as near starvation as his old master. I never beheld two more pitiable objects since I have made these woods my home, and I never desire to again."

Lucelle listened with beating heart and swelling bosom to the story about the old Indian. She was so much affected at his recital, that the tears chased each other down her cheeks in rapid succession. With all her high, ambitious notions, and aspirations for fame and distinction, she had a heart full of tender sensibilities, and overflowing with the milk of human kindness.

"I thought the Indians could always get game enough to keep them from starving," she said, in a voice choked with sobbing.

"They do generally," replied her father. "But I remember that was a very extraordinary time. It had been snowing and blowing for five days without any cessation at all, and besides, the weather was very cold, and the game very scarce, as it always is on such occasions. Even partridges will plunge into the snow and bury themselves beneath the white covering to get out of the way of the storm. I have sometimes travelled a whole day and not seen even a squirrel to shoot at. But I was always careful to carry with me a pretty good portion of food to guard against what might happen."

"Oh, father, Turok says the British soldiers are coming to take the fort," she said.

"How does he know that?" he inquired. "I have had some fears of it recently."

"He heard of it from some Indians at the head of the lake," she replied.

"Well, Lucelle, we must be quiet and be as friendly to one party as to another," he said. "The Indians will never hurt us, and I don't see why the British should, if they should take the fort, any more than the French have. Perhaps some of the soldiers might attempt to rob me, if they thought I had any money, but they will not suppose that, and we shall be safe; besides, the officers would punish them if they should do violence to an old man. They would be troubled to find the money, if they should break in upon us."

"I'm more afraid of the British than I am of the French, or of the Indians," she said. "I don't like them. If they should attempt to rob us, they should find out how well I can fire a gun."

"You wouldn't shoot them, would you?" he asked, smiling at the erect posture she assumed, and at her dark, flashing eyes.

"As quick as I would pop over a wild duck," she answered.

"That would be murder," said the old hunter.

"Well, don't they murder, and why shouldn't they be murdered?" she inquired.

"It would be right to shoot them in self-defence, but if they don't trouble us, we will let them alone," he said. "It will make but little difference to us, who commands the fort, whether French or English."

"You're a Frenchman, father, and why don't you take sides with the French?" she asked.

"The French government did not use me well before I left the country," he replied. "The king and his ministers would not pardon me of a crime of which I was accused and found guilty."

"A crime!" she repeated, in much surprise. "Were you ever guilty of crime!"

"No, I was not guilty, but was convicted on the testimony of a witness who swore falsely," he replied. "No, no, Lucelle. I was not guilty, and Heaven knows I was not."

"Of what crime were you convicted?" she anxiously inquired.

"Of forging my brother's name," he replied. "But that brother pursued me with the revenge of a devil rather than with the feelings of a brother. He wanted me to leave Paris, and he knew, if I was convicted of a crime, I should leave the country as soon as my sentence expired. For three years was I kept in prison.

At the expiration of that time, I was released from prison, and then fled from my country."

"Why should your brother be so cruel ?" she asked.

" Our father was aged, and my brother thought he could not continue long, and so he took that method to get rid of me, that he might have all our father's estate after his decease. I became disgusted with the government, and with my own kinsmen, and came over to the new world."

"You never told me so much of your life before," said Lucelle.

" True, I never have," he replied. " And it were well, perhaps, if I had not told you."

" Oh, father, I'm glad you have done so," she replied. " Do you ever expect to go back to France ?"

" Why do you ask me, Lucelle?" he inquired. " What put that into your head?"

" That young Indian told me," she answered. " He did not say you were actually going to take that journey, but inferred from what you said to him that you sometimes seriously thought of it."

" That young fellow has a good memory, and seems to take a deep interest in whatever concerns us," said the old man. " I do remember saying something to him about visiting the land of my birth ; but I had forgotten the circumstance. Turok is really our friend, and so was his father. If he were not an Indian, I should be almost tempted to let him have you for his wife."

" Perhaps he would not have me," she replied.

" Perhaps not !" repeated her father, ironically. " No doubt he loves you more than any other person does, except your own father. And indeed he is worthy of your highest reward, but the races ought not to mingle their blood. Let them remain separate and distinct. This young Indian will always be our friend, for he will never forget the act of kindness I did to his father. Let him be our friend. The time may come when his services may be valuable to us."

" I shall do nothing, father, to forbid his friendship, neither shall I conduct myself towards him in such a manner as to encourage his hopes that I would become his wife. That I like him I candidly confess, but love him I never can."

" Oh? Lucelle, you have relieved my heart of a great burden," said her father. " For several months I have watched your movements as well as his, and sometimes I feared you might love him ; but now I am entirely satisfied. Seek his company as much as you please, but do not encourage him to hope for anything beyond what friendship can give. Deceive him not ; for I should rather see you sink in yonder lake to rise no more, than to know that you have deceived such a young man. Humble as my situation in life is, I'm too proud to have my daughter become an Indian's wife."

" And your daughter is too proud to have an Indian for her husband," replied Lucelle, standing erect, and gazing proudly into her father's withered face.

" Unlike the white man, Turok will never urge you to a compliance with his wishes, and I doubt whether he will ever disclose his passion to you," he said. " He will keep the flame shut up in his own heart, and there let it burn."

" I hope it will ; but could wish it might go out entirely if any does burn in his heart," replied Lucelle. " While Turok and I were talking at the landing, that officer Delano was standing not far off and gazing most intently upon us. I don't like his appearance at all. I've found him before staring at me when I've been on the shore of the lake."

" You must beware of him, Lucelle," said her father. " He would ruin you if he could, but I have not many fears, for I think you can withstand all his arts. Don't you think you can ?"

" I do indeed, father," she replied. " He can never have any power over me, I like Turok better than I do him, and would tell him so, if he should name love to me."

"I will go out and kill some partridges or some other game," said the father. "You had better remain in the hous , a the weather is extremely warm."

The old hunter took his gun and started out into the woods, while Lucelle went a few paces from the lodge to visit her mother's grave. She often visited this sacred spot, which was situated on the side of a small hill near the brook. It was a beautiful and romantic place, commanding a fine view of the lake, and the scenery upon the opposite side. A small block of limestone marked the spot where were deposited the earthly remains of her mother and two children. Near the head of the grave were a little bunch of wild flowers which Lucelle transplanted there and culti- vated with her own hands. Almost every day through the warm dry season, she would fetch water from the brook in a vessel made from birch bark, and water the flowers. Young Turok made this little watering-pot, and gave it to her in the early part of the season. It was made in an oval form, with a strip of birch bark nicely punched with holes, fastened across one end, through which the fair Lucelle let the water trickle upon her flowers. It was beautifully stained with bright red and purple colors, and the handle, or rather bail, was neatly carved from white ash wood. This was also stained with different colours, and some fine moss nicely fitted to the part designed for the hand. The whole was a very ingenious piece of work, and cost the young Indian several days of steady labour. But he performed the task with a light heart, and exercised all his mechanical skill and ingenuity, which were by no means inconsiderable. He gave it to her about the middle of May, and she had kept it very choice, using it for no other purpose than watering her flowers, and hanging it carefully up in a particular place in the lodge after using it.

When she went to the grave, she took this vessel with her for the purpose of watering her flowers, and just as she was sprinkling them with this little shower of rain, Lieutenant Delano made his appearance at a few paces distant from her. She did not at first discover him, but continued the process of gently watering her delicate flowers, while he stood, partially concealed by a bunch of bushes, silently watching her.

"Grow on, bright flowers, for the season is fast approaching when your beau- tiful leaves will be nipped and withered by the frost," she said, in a voice loud enough for the young officer to hear, while she was pouring the pure brook water upon them. "I, too, shall have my season, but it will not be long, for time flies rapidly away. Oh, that I could do something to make my name known beyond these woods ! And yet I love these scenes, and especially this sacred spot. Oh, how I should desire to carry it with me if I should leave my native forest, and these flowers, this brook, and this beautifal watering-pot too, which young Turok so ingeniously made, and generously gave to me."

" She mentions the name of that young Indian who is so often with her," said Delano to himself. " My suspicions, I fear, will turn out to be true. She loves him. No, no. Such a beautiful creature can never love an Indian. And yet Turok is really handsomer in face and form than nineteen-twentieths of the young white men. But he must not marry her. She must be mine. What a fool I am that I have not declared my passion for her long ere this ! I may have deferred it already too long. She's proud, there can be no doubt, for her coun- tenance and every motion of her beautiful form show it. To her pride, then, will I appeal, and if truth be not sufficient to win her heart, I can utter some false- hoods. I'm poor, I know, but then I can say I'm rich, and that she shall live in splendour. I must approach and have some talk with her. This opportunity must not pass unimproved. Her father is not here, and the young Indian has gone. Now is my time."

As these thoughts chased each other through his mind, he stopped from be- hind the bushes which had partially concealed him from her view, and her eyes fell on him ; but she did not suddenly start, nor let her watering-pot fall from her hands. She was not afraid of him, although he was an officer, and therefore she continued to water her flowers until he approached within arm's length of her.

" God day to you, Lucelle," he said, gazing into her dark eyes, and wishing to imprint a kiss upon her full red lips. " It is a beautiful day, but rather warm and dry. Your flowers would droop, I conclude, in such weather as this unless you watered them. I've often looked at those flowers and supposed they must be watered often, they appear so fresh and beautiful."

" Yes, sir, I take great pleasure in washing the dust from their leaves, and refreshing their roots with the pure water from the brook," she replied.

" It is a beautiful employment most surely," he replied. " By the appearance of the place there is a grave here, I conclude."

" The grave of my mother, sir," she answered. " I visit this place quite often. I love to come out here early in the morning, and listen to the birds as they sing in the branches of the trees. My mother was once very fond of the music of birds. She has often led me out on the banks of that little brook when I was a little girl, just big enough to toddle along by her side, to listen to the sweet songs of these warblers. Oh, those days were happy ones indeed. I then had no aspirations for anything beyond these scenes."

" Do you now wish for anything the woods do not furnish ?" he inquired.

" For nearly eighteen years I have gazed upon this forest and this lake, and is it strange, sir, that I should sometimes sigh for a change ?" she asked casting her dark eyes upon him as she would read his inmost soul.

" Surely it is not : but it would be most singularly strange if you did not wish for other sights besides these which the forest affords," he replied. " True, my sweet girl, you adore these wild and romantic scenes, but then you might shine as an ornament in more civilised and highly cultivated life. You transplanted those flowers at the head of your mother's grave. They once grew in another place, and yet they look fresh and beautiful here, as when you first took them from their native bed."

" Oh yes, sir, I think they look even more blooming and fresh than they did then," she replied. " I was very careful when I dug the roots up to remove considerable earth with them ; besides I never let them lack water, especially when the air is hot and dry."

" So you would look more fresh and blooming if you were transplanted from your native forest to some city where you could figure in fashionable life," he said. " What pure brook water is to these flowers, would be a fine house and rich apparel to you. Your beauty would adorn any palace, even the most fashionable one in Paris."

" Were you ever in Paris ?" she inquired.

" Indeed, my dear girl, that's my native city," he replied. " After the war is over, I expect to return there again. I left many gay friends there, besides a very handsome fortune. But I thought more of the glory of France than I did of all these things. When her power is fully established among her colonies here, and her rights fully acknowledged, I shall go to my native city—to my beloved Paris, and then spend the remainder of my days in ease and affluence."

" I wish my father would go to that city," she said. " That was his native place."

" I thought so by his motions and looks," he replied. " The life in the wood which he has lived, nor his age, has entirely blotted out all the marks of a city life which were placed upon him in his younger days. His still easy and graceful manners show that he was well bred. He received impressions in youth which old age can never erase. You too have many of his motions, but you did not learn them in the city, but rather from his example. Women and men are too imitative creatures. I have had it often upon my mind to ask your father where his native place is, for I thought he must have lived in other places besides the forest. I'm now satisfied. I always feel a peculiar gratification when I find my conjectures are correct. I have the vanity to believe that I can judge a man's character very nearly correct after I have seen him a few times, and pardon me when I say I think I can a woman's too. I had some acquaintance with your sex in times past."

"Perhaps you have a beautiful wife in Paris to moan over your absence," said Lucelle, feeling some curiosity to learn whether he was a married man or not.

"Oh, no, I was never married nor in love before I came into this wilderness," he replied.

"Well, surely you could not have seen anything to wake that tender passion in your heart since you have come here," she said, while a pleasant smile played over her beautiful face.

"Not until I saw the wild flower before me," he replied, returning her smile.

"Then you love these flowers at the head of my mother's grave as well as I do," she said, making him believe she thought he alluded to the flowers instead of herself. "I'm very fond of the wild flowers which grow in the forests. I always stop to gaze upon them when I happen to pass them in my walks in the woods."

"I did not speak of flowers, but of a flower," he replied, emphasising the last word on the sentence, and shrewdly looking at her.

"Then you have seen one more beautiful than all these, have you?" she inquired. "When I found these, I thought they were more beautiful than any I had seen, so I selected and transplanted them here. If I could have seen the beautiful one you speak of, I presume I should have chosen that."

"Did you never see yourself in the mirror surface of the lake when you have been gliding over its waters in your light canoe?" he asked, assuming a very cunning look.

"Oh, yes, quite often when no winds ripple its fair bosom," she replied.

"Then have you seen that same flower of which I spoke," he answered, drawing towards her, and laying his hand upon the watering-pot she still held. He would have been glad to seize her hand, but she was not yet ripe for that; at any rate he felt as if it might be advancing a single step too far; therefore he contented himself by placing his hand on the vessel very near hers.

She turned her deep black eyes upon him in such a gaze that he was glad he did not venture to press her hand as his first impulse prompted him to do. Her lips made no reply to this indirect declaration of his passion, but she stood erect and silent. He felt as if she intended to rebuke him by her silence and manners without the aid of words. He thought for the moment he should rather face the British army than such a pair of black eyes. He was really embarrassed for a short time. At last the thought struck him that as his hand was on the watering-pot he would, by some means or other, take it, examine it, and praise it.

"This is a beautiful vessel to water your flowers with," he said, taking it from her hand, and looking at it with apparent admiration. "Did you make and paint it so elegantly? If you did, you must be quite a genius."

"Oh, no, I did not make it," she replied. "I have not ingenuity enough to make such a beautiful article. It would take more ready and better practised fingers than mine. Young Turok made, and gave it to me last spring, and I've used it ever since, but very carefully. It is a very pretty present. Don't you think so?"

"The article itself is very well, but the donor is not so engaging," he replied. "I don't have a very high opinion of the Indians. I've seen too much of them to place much confidence in them. They are a treacherous race and full of deceit."

"Young Turok is not treacherous and deceitful, is he?" she inquired.

"I suppose you think he is not," he replied. "But I wouldn't trust him nor any other of the copper-coloured race out of my sight. At one hour they'll appear very fair to your face, and at the next take your scalp off. You cannot trust them with safety. Lucelle, I wish to ask you one question."

"You can ask me two if you please," she said. "But you must allow me to act my own pleasure in answering them."

"Oh, certainly," he replied, softening down a little when he saw how prompt, ready, and resolute she was. "Do you love that young Indian?"

"Why do you ask me that question?" she inquired, very indifferently. "Have you ever thought that I did?"

"I have not been able to find out what I thought," he replied. "He has been with you often, and you have received presents from him. And that is not all. You seem to prize this birch bark watering-pot very highly, and to take very special care of it. This I have just had from your own lips. Now can you blame me for having some suspicions that you and he are on familiar terms with one another?"

"I attach no blame to you at all," she replied. "You have a right to your own thoughts, and I have a right to give my heart to whom I please. Turok is my friend, but not my lover. He has never declared his love to me. And I'm quite certain he never will. Humble in life as I am, and worthy as Turok may be, I could never assent to marry him. He and I belong to two separate and distinct races. And I feel as if these two races ought to be kept separate and distinct. You know my mind."

"I do indeed, and glad am I to hear you thus express yourself," he replied. "You have too many charms, and too much personal beauty to spend your days in an Indian's wigwam. You were made for more polished society, and to move in more splendid circles. Would you not choose such a life, if it were in your power?"

"I know I'm proud and ambitious, but it would be folly for me, situated as I am, to expect such a life," she replied.

"It is in your power," he said, seizing her hand, and suddenly bringing it in contact with his lips.

"Forbear!" she said, withdrawing her hand, and suddenly leaving him standing by her mother's grave motionless as a statue. A moment before he kissed her hand his heart was full of hope that she would be easily conquered, but now a cloud came suddenly and unexpectedly over his prospects. Standing a few moments and gazing upon her retreating form until he saw her enter her father's lodge, he turned upon his heel, and repaired to the fort, much dispirited.

CHAPTER III.

RUMOURS became ripe among the officers and soldiers of Ticonderoga Fort that the British and provincial troops, under the command of General Amherst, were on the march through the woods by the way of Lake George. An attack was expected, and much excitement prevailed within the garrison. Some of the officers were of opinion that the best policy was to set fire to the fort, and flee to Crown Point, a position farther down the lake, where they imagined they could more successfully resist the British forces. Others were of a different opinion, and thought it best to defend their present position. It was not yet certainly known to them that the enemy was on the march for the purpose of beseiging the fort, although some friendly Indians had told them that such was the fact.

While they were under the excitement which these rumours naturally produced, Lieutenant Delano was despatched with twenty men to scour the woods in every direction within ten miles of the fort, and bring intelligence in case any evidence of the enemy's movements was discovered, tending to confirm the tidings which the Indians had previously brought. It was the next day after Delano had his interview with Lucelle de la Motte at her mother's grave, when he was ordered upon this reconnoitring expedition. The night previous had been a restless one for him. This meeting with the fair Lucelle had inflamed his heart, and fully convinced him that he was absolutely and decidedly in love with the beautiful maid of the lake; but how to win her was the great question which absorbed his whole soul. He thought much more of securing her than he did of defending the fort. He fancied he had, by his arts and false stories about his birth, standing, property and prospects, made a favourable impression upon her heart. He thought he had discovered on her countenance expressions of manifest delight and approbation at the recital of his false stories. To him she appeared ambitious and aspiring. Her father, too, he thought was proud and ambitious, and would approve his suit. The only cloud which he now saw overshadowing his prospects was occasioned by her manner of leaving him at her mother's grave. He did not like the symptom of that; for just as he had raised her beautiful hand to his burning lips, and was about to imprint upon it a passionate kiss, she fled to her father's lodge. This circumstance he dwelt upon during the whole of a sleepless night, placing upon it a variety of constructions, sometimes favourable, and again not so favourable to his wishes as he might desire. Upon the whole, however, he forced himself into a belief that she almost loved him. With these views and feelings, he seized a few moments before he started at the head of his score of men on the reconnoitring excursion, and repaired to the old hunter's lodge. He found the old occupant and his fair daughter at breakfast.

"Excuse me, my dear friends, for intruding upon you at this unseasonable hour, but being about to scour the woods in our vicinity to see if the enemy gave any signs of approach, I thought I would just run down and see you a moment before I started," he said, as he entered the lodge.

"No apology, lieutenant, is necessary," replied De la Motte. "My lodge is always open for friends at all hours of the day, and even if an enemy should enter it, I would endeavour to make him so welcome that he would go away my friend. I wish these wars could be brought to a close, and leave us all happy and peaceful."

"I wish so too, and then I could return to my beloved France again," replied the young officer.

"Ah! then you came from France, did you?" inquired the old man. "Lucelle was just saying before you came in that you were born in Paris."

"Did she condescend to speak of me thus early in the morning?" he asked, assuming a very pleasant manner, and smiling most graciously.

"Ah! she dreamt of me, perhaps, last night, or I should not this morning have become the subject of her conversation and thoughts," he said within himself. "I was right. She does love me, and her leaving me so suddenly at her mother's grave was only the effect of natural diffidence and maidenly modesty. I'll have her, and revel in her charms. She smiles now at my presence, and seems glad, although she endeavours to conceal every demonstration of it as much as possible. But those sparkling dark eyes will speak out the feelings of her soul in spite of all her efforts to conceal them. She is most lovely, angelic creature. She must be mine."

"Oh, yes, lieutenant, she has been talking about you a good deal this morning," replied the father. "And she had something to say last night."

"What did she say last night?" anxiously inquired the officer. "I should esteem myself most happy to know that she not only spoke of me last evening and this morning, but also that I was the subject of her dreams during the night; for surely I dreamt of her, and could not be easy until I had seen her before my departure. I may never return alive again; for we who are obliged to explore the forests in search of the enemy's movements, are liable to be picked off at any moment by some unfriendly and savage Indian. We have no security for our lives in these dangerous times; but the glory of our beloved France calls us to the field, and bid us face danger in defence of her honour and her rights."

He made the above remarks for the double purpose of making the fair maid believe that he was very courageous, and also of exciting her fears for his safety.

He looked at her sharply, to see if he could discover any symptoms of alarm for his safety in her countenance, but apt as he was to construe her movements in his favour, yet he was now forced to believe that she did not express any extraordinary symptoms of alarm. This was a damper to his feelings, but still his passion for her in some degree blinded his eyes, and he attributed this apparent indifference on her part to her cunning and shrewdness.

"You ask what Lucelle said last evening," replied the old Frenchman. "I will tell you."

"Nay, father!" she exclaimed, "do not tell him, I intreat you."

The young officer's curiosity was now excited to the highest pitch. He had no doubt but she had been telling her father how much she loved him. His heart eat quick, and his bosom swelled with pleasing emotions. It was a moment in which he seemed to live months.

No. 3.

"Ah! now, Lucelle don't attempt to seal up your father's lips, if y₁ do keep your own closed," said Delano, smiling upon her most sweetly, and bowing as politely as any Frenchman ever did on any occasion. "Out with it, Monsieur de la Motte, and let my heart pulsate while her fair cheeks are crimsoned over with modest blushes. I love your daughter, and have long cherished for her such an affectionate regard as I never yet felt for the fairest belle in all Paris. Let me but know that she reciprocates that affection, and I am of all men the most happy."

"Ah! my good friend, Lieutenant Delano, young maidens will have their fancies and their freaks in the wild forests as well as in the polished cities," replied the old hunter. "It is their nature, and it will show itself in spite of all outward circumstances. The female heart is a strange book, and wise is he who can read and understand it."

"I'm aware of it, my dear sir," replied the young officer. "And fortunate indeed is he who loves her who loves him. I was once placed in no very enviable position before I left Paris. A beautiful girl of one of the best families in France fell in love with me, but I could not return her affection. I regretted that, but I was not in fault myself. I made no efforts to win her heart, but she gave it voluntarily, and before I was aware of it."

"If she was so beautiful and belonged to such a high family, why did you not reciprocate her affection?" modestly inquired Lucelle.

"Ah! dear girl. there was that indefinable something lacking in her person or manners which my heart sighed for," he replied. "What it was I could never divine unless it was her eyes."

"What of her eyes?" inquired Lucelle. Where they not handsome and expresive?"

"They were generally thought to be very handsome and expressive, but they were a light blue," he replied, fondly gazing into the bewildering depths of her dark orbs, which were now lighted up with peculiar brilliancy. At any rate he thought so.

"Very well said, and a handsome compliment to Lucelle's black eyes," thought her father. "If he loves her, and what he says of himself be true, he would make a fine match for Lucelle. But I must know more about him before I give him too much encouragement. I should be pleased to have Lucelle marry a rich man of Paris ; for I intend to return there one of these days when I collect money enough to carry me to the city of my birth. Perhaps this young officer has money as well as rank."

These thoughts were running rapidly through the old hunter's head, while visions of splendour were floating in the imagination of his ambitious daughter.

For a few moments silence reigned in that old habitation, and no one seemed disposed to break it. Both father and daughter were changed in their feelings towards the French officer. Lucelle had never fancied him, but now she felt as if an union with him might enable her to realise some of her dreams of happiness and splendour. Delano with eagle eyes watched the workings of their countenances, and flattered himself that matters were tending to a very favourable issue. The character he assumed was entirely false, for he had never seen Paris in his life, nor crossed the broad Atlantic. He was born of low parentage in Cape Breton, but by dint of great exertions he had obtained a lieutenancy in the army. His heart, was corrupt, and notwithstanding his great pretensions to a love for France, he was ready at any moment to abandon the service of his country, if he thought he could improve his condition by so doing. It had been whispered among the officers and soldiers of the fort that old De la Motte had accumulated, by the sale of furs, a considerable sum of money. This rumour he was not a stranger to, and added somewhat to the charms of Lucelle; still he loved this beautiful maid for her own charms, aside from any influence that gold might produce, and was determined to have her at all hazards.

"It is strange how a little matter will influence the heart!" he continued. "I think it very possible I might have loved that beautiful Parisian belle, if her eyes had been somewhat of a deeper blue, and her hair and complexion had been not quite so *blonde*. I have always been told that I am rather particular and fastidous, and I suppose I am. That young lady thought so no doubt. When I left Paris for the glory of France, she was in great distress of mind, so some of my friends told me."

"And have you not since heard from her?" inquired Lucelle, in a voice whose accents told how deep was her sympathy for the young lady who had fallen so hopelessly in love with him.

"Oh, Lucelle, I did hope you would spare me from answering such a question," he replied, assuming an air of seriousness. and gazingly into her face. "But I will answer you frankly and honestly. I have heard from her. In less than a year from the time I left my native city; she pined away and died of a broken heart."

A tear stood trembling in Lucelle's dark eye, which the young officer watched, with peculiar sensations of delight, for he fancied that the big drop furnished strong evidence that she believed his false story.

"Yes ; my dear Lucelle, she died in all her youth and beauty, went down to an untimely grave," he continued, wiping one eye with his handkerchief, as if a tear had started, and fondly looking with the other into her countenance to see the effect of his well-varnished tale. "But no blame could attach to me, for I was innocent. I could not return her love. After I heard of her death, I sent authority to my agent in Paris to erect a marble monument over her remains, and to expend upon it one thousand francs. I felt as if I could do no less than that, under all the circumstances of the case."

"And was the monument erected?" inquired the old hunter, looking sharply into the officer's face to see if he could discover any evidence of his lying.

"It was finished this very summer, and erected over her grave," he replied. "In a letter from my agent he informs me that the monument is visited by thousands of the citizens of Paris, and the papers extol me to the skies for the generous and liberal act. He further says, when I return to Paris the friends and relatives of the young lady will greet me with ten thousand smiles of approbation, and even beg for the privilege of carrying me into the city in triumph upon their shoulders. I should like to be in Paris this day, but I should humbly decline all such public demonstrations of joy."

"You did well," said Lucelle. "But, oh, how I pity that young lady! Has she parents living?"

"She has a mother." he replied. "Her father has been dead several years. She was an only child, and much beloved by all who knew her. I have often thought it very strange and mysterious that I could not love her, but now the mystery is solved."

"How so?" innocently inquired Lucelle.

"When I first saw you, dear girl, I then knew why I could not love her," he replied.

"I cannot see the reason for that," said Lucelle. "How is it?"

"Because she did not resemble you," he answered. "It has been decreed by the fates that my heart must love such as you, and you alone. I now see it all clearly. It has been a matter of surprise to me that I did not fall in love with some of the ladies of Paris ; for I mingled in the society of many beautiful ones ; but the reason is obvious enough now—I had not seen your face and form then. I feel that you were created for me in the order of Providence, and this impression came over me when my eyes first fell upon you. It would strike my friends and acquaintances in Paris very singularly if I should carry back with me a wild flower from the forests of the new world, after I had passed by so many cultivated ones of the old. I have been, perhaps, too frank in the declaration of my feelings, but, Lucelle, excuse me if I have, and you, Monsieur de la Motte. Ah, I hope to be forgiven by you also, if I have said aught to offend you."

"You've not offended me, dear sir," replied De la Motte. "When do you think of returning to Paris?"

"Oh, sir, I trust I shall be able to do so in the fall, or in the course of next winter," he replied. "Do you not intend to go too? If your lovely daughter would consent to accompany me, I should be pleased to have you return with us. Indeed I shouldhardly be willing to leave you behind, and I'm quite sure Lucelle would not."

"I should be unwilling to go anywhere and leave my father alone in this wilderness," she replied. "He is now advanced in years, and will soon be unable to roam the forests as he has in years past."

"True, Lucelle, most true," said her father. "Although I'm yet hearty and strong, and can track the otter and beaver with any of the young men, yet I feel the infirmities of age creeping upon me, and soon I must give up this hunting life."

"I dare say you have found it a profitable, although it may have been a laborious one," said the officer, wishing to ascertain indirectly how much money the old hunter had got together by the sale of his furs.

"It has not been, I trust, without some profit," replied the old man. "I have worked hard, and been quite economical.

"If rumour is to be relied on, you have accumulated several thousand francs," said Delano, feeling curious to ascertain the exact amount, if he could do it without seeming too anxious in the premises.

"Ah! rumour is as uncertain a judge as fortune herself," replied De la Motte. "I have taken the skins from a great number of otters and beavers, and they have always brought the silver and gold. It always gives me a very pleasing impulse, and a warm glow about the heart, to go out on a cold, frosty morning, and find all my traps filled with game. It is an exceeding pleasant sight, I can assure you."

"Not so much pleasure in merely looking at the unfortunate creatures in your traps, as the money you see ahead," said the officer, smiling, and feeling quite certain that he should get at something near the amount of the old hunter's money.

"Very true, lieutenant," said the old man, returning his smile. "I don't suppose I should be at the trouble of catching the sleek fellows, if it were not for their warm coverings. It might do well enough for a beginner to catch them for sport, but after he had followed the business for twenty-five years, as I have, he would not expose himself to heats and colds merely for the sport of the thing."

"Have you followed hunting twenty-five years?" inquired the young lieutenant.

"Yes, it will be twenty-six years since I commenced such a course of life," he replied.

"And have you been lucky as a trapper during all that time?" inquired Delano.

"The Indians say I have beat any two of them," he answered. "Yes, I have been very lucky. I suppose I have no reason to complain."

"Father has worked hard enough to retire from the woods, I think," said Lucelle. "But he thinks he hasn't money enough yet."

"If he has not enough to carry him to Paris, he may go with me, and I will pay the expenses of the voyage," said the lieutenant, swelling up, and looking quite big.

"Oh, I suppose I have enough to pay for my voyage, and have a few francs left," said the old man winking slily, as if he was willing the young officer should know that his coffers were pretty well filled with silver and gold.

"Some think you have quite a large sum, and others think you have not," said Delano. "I overheard a couple of soldiers talking about it to-day. I was very much amused with their dialogue. One said he had no doubt but that you had laid up in your life five thousand francs, and the other remarked that he didn't believe you had five hundred. They became quite warm upon the subject. It amused me very much to see how easily a dispute will sometimes arise between two soldiers about a subject in which they have not the least personal interest whatever."

"I don't understand why they should have made my hard-earned money a subject of their conversation or dispute," said the old man. "They don't intend to rob me, do they?"

"Not so long as I have any command over them," answered the officer. "They should be shot if they attempted anything of that kind. I presume, however, there is no danger of our soldiers doing such deeds. They are too much afraid of punishment for that."

"I didn't suppose there was any danger," said the old man; "I spoke of it more in fun than in earnest."

"Do you keep your money in silver?" inquired the officer. "If you do, you will have a pile of it one of these days, so big that you could not carry it with you."

"It is principally yellow," replied the old hunter, smiling. "I'm thinking rust has not yet corrupted it, although some of the pieces have been in my possession a quarter of a century. The pile is not so large yet but Lucelle and I could shoulder and lug it off."

"How much have you, do you think?" inquired Delano, apparently indifferent. "No, no, my good friend, I was wrong to ask you. You need not answer the question, unless you are perfectly willing. It is a subject which does not concern me. I should be glad if you had enough of the metal to fill our largest cannon. It is your daughter, and not your money I'm after. I've gold enough to pay the expenses of my voyage to Paris three times over, and when I arrive in that beloved and well-remembered city, I shall be flush. The letter of my agent says my estate has been very productive since my absence."

"I have no objections to answering your question," said De la Motte, "I would not, however, wish to make the matter too public."

"Oh, sir, you can rely upon me. I shall never divulge any secret which you may please to entrust me with," replied Delano, feeling his ear itch to hear how much gold the old man had stowed away in his coffers, and yet assuming an indifference about it to cover up his real designs.

"Father can tell you how much he has to a sou, for not a week passes over his head that he does not count it over and over again," said Lucelle, laughing.

"Well, Lucelle, you may laugh," said her father. "I do love to count it over, I like the looks of it, because it is the very thing which will convey us down the Iroquois, and across the ocean. It makes me laugh too when I think of it."

"Not to be blamed for that by any means," said Delano. "Gold is a very convenient article; I have always found it so, at any rate. True, you have not seen the real use of it while hoarding it up, except by anticipation."

"I have during the last twenty-five years accumulated nearly eight thousand francs," said the old man. "I have thought when I made the sum ten thousand, I should cross the ocean and let Lucelle see Paris and all its fine things."

"Eight thousand francs!" replied the young officer over to himself. "Eight thousand francs! Well, I must have the fingering of that sum before any part of it, or its owner, reaches Paris. I'll have this girl and the money, if I have to make a ladder of the old hunter's dead body to reach them."

For the first time the thought of murdering the old hunter entered his soul, and dark, indeed, was that thought!

"You have been exceedingly lucky and accumulated a very pretty little sum," replied Delano, appearing quite indifferent as if he thought the sum was not very great.

"A pretty little sum!" said the old man within himself. "It does not appear so large to him as it does to me. But let him expend twenty five years of hard labour to accumulate as much, and I will swear for it that it will not look so very small to him. He has, perhaps, five times that amount, but then he never earned it as I have, by hard knocks and exposure to all sorts of weather."

"Yes, I have been fortunate, but I suppose the sum looks small to you who have many times the amount," said the old hunter. "But you have not got your money as I have mine. Your money, perhaps, was left you by a rich father, while mine was caught in traps of my own setting."

"True, my estate was left me by my father, and consequently I did not have much hand in accumulating it," he replied. "But it has been some trouble to take care of it. I have left it in good hands since I took up arms for my country, and it has been rapidly gaining since I enlisted in the service. I hope to be able one of these days to enjoy the good of it in Paris. After I return, I shall feel contented to settle down and be at ease, especially if your daughter will consent to live with me. Without her society, riches, fine houses, and beautiful gardens, and a splendid equipage, will never afford me pleasure. She has won my heart, and, strange to you as it may appear, I have passed by all other ladies without ever having my heart touched with the talisman of love. This work has been reserved for your daughter, and most essentially has she done it. Had I been told when I left Paris that some nymph of these wild forests would pierce my heart with her dark eyes, I should have laughed in the teller's face, and treated him with scorn and contempt for his folly. But the work has been most successfully done, and I stand here this morning to declare and acknowledge it. My opinion of love matters has undergone a change since I came to these wilds. Once I scorned the idea that matches were made in heaven, but now I fully believe in the philosophy which teaches such a doctrine. If it is not so, why did I come all the way here to fall in love? The doctrine is true. I have the evidence of its truth within my own breast. I'm a living witness of its truth."

"I have some such notions myself," said the old man. "When I first saw Lucelle's mother, it seemed to me that she looked different from any other woman I ever saw."

"That's it exactly," hurriedly answered the young officer, feeling more and more encouraged the longer he stayed. "I felt just so the first time my eyes fell on Lucelle. There was something in the form of her face, the expression of her eyes, or in her easy graceful motions, which I never saw in any other female. The first time I saw her, was when she jumped from the canoe upon the rock at the mouth of the brook. But she did not know I was looking at her, I was concealed behind a tree several rods distant from her."

"When was that?" inquired Lucelle, feeling somewhat flattered at the young officer's remark in spite of all her efforts to guard against it.

"It was more than two months ago, soon after I received orders to station myself at Ticonderoga fort," he replied. "Well do I remember the circumstance, and may I hope that I never shall regret its occurrence?"

Silence now reigned in the little room where they were assembled, no one wishing to break it first. The young officer stood looking at the fair Lucelle, she at him, and the old hunter at both of them. By his art, cunning, and lies, he had evidently made a favourable impression upon both father and daughter. Paris with all its finery and splendour floated before their vision. He saw how matters were working, and was highly gratified. The eight thousand francs in gold had a charm for him, as well as the deep, dark eyes of the beautiful maid of the lake. He thought the time would soon come when he should throw off his regimentals, and become the possessor of Lucelle and her father's money. The glory of France he had spoken of so enthusiastically, and all the splendours of Parisian life he had so much expatiated upon, were now forgotten. He said to himself that he would quit the service of his country as soon as he could do so without danger to himself. The liberties of France, or her colonial rights, he cared not a farthing for, and never did. He had now overstayed his time, and was anxious to go back to the fort, but no answer had been given to his last question. He began to grow impatient, and the old hunter saw his impatience.

"You can hope as all men do said the father. "At some future day we will talk over this matter again

"I thank you kindly, sir, and you, dear Lucelle, let me leave with you a token of my purest love until I return," he replied, kissing her hand, and leaving the room.

CHAPTER IV.

"How far are we from the fort now, comrades?" inquired Delano, after having travelled round in the woods some three or four hours in search of the enemy's movements.

"We are not more than six miles in straight line from the fort," replied one of his men, who was much better acquainted with the lay of the land than the questioner was. "I know this little brook well; it runs near old Motte's lodge, and empties into the lake where he hauls in his canoe. I have seen that Lucelle, with her long curling hair, and black eyes, haul up the canoe a young Indian made for her, into the same brook many a time."

"Then you have seen the old hunter's daughter, have you?" inquired Delano.

"Many a time, before I ever turned soldier," replied the man, whose name was Joseph Prideaux, a smart, active fellow, and much better qualified to be the leader of this reconnoitering party than Delano was. "She's a beautiful creature. Oh, Jehu! if you could have seen her when I did, about six weeks ago, you would have thought she was a real mermaid."

"Why, under what circumstances did you see her that made you think of a mermaid?" asked the young officer, in much anxiety.

"In a swimming in the lake, and a handsomer fish I never saw," replied Prideaux. "Ah! she cut through the water like a trout, and dived like a water-witch. I stood on a bluff of rocks at some distance from her, and gazed with delight upon her form and motions. There was a little ripple on the water at the time, and her long curling hair looked as if there were a dozen black water-snakes swimming after her head and ready to swallow it. Oh, thought I, if I had a hook that I could catch such a fish as that with, I'd never fish again in any brook or lake. But it's no use, she's too shy to bite at any hook except an Indian's."

"What do you mean by that?" anxiously inquired Delano, with a beating heart and swelling bosom.

"Mean by that!" echoed Jo, as he was familiarly called; "why, I mean just what I said. They say that she has bit at a young Indian's hook, and that he has caught her. Well, young Turok is a devilish smart, ingenious fellow, if he is an Indian. He's straight as an arrow, active as a deer, and strong as a bear. I should hate to fall into his hands if he were angry."

"She love an Indian," exclaimed Delano, apparently in wrath. "Why, Jo, you talk like a fool. If she is so beautiful as you say she is, do you think she would marry an Indian? Nonsense! man. She'll never be guilty of that."

"Perhaps she will not; but I've seen them together many a time in the woods," said Jo, somewhat excited at the sharp rebuke of the officer. "I once saw a trial of skill between them in shooting a grey squirrel upon the top of a tall dry pine-tree with the bow and arrow. Turok fired first, and cut off a part of the poor squirrel's tail; but that only frightened him a little, and made him change his position on the limb of the tree. He laid as close to the limb as he could get, and looked slily down at his tormentors, as if he wished they would let his tail alone. Lucelle drew her bow most gracefully, while a smile played over her pretty face, and her bosom heaved with pleasant emotions, and off went the arrow with the speed of lightning. It struck the squirrel's head exactly half way between his eyes, and down he came plump into the fair creature's sun-bonnet, which she held out to receive him the moment she let the arrow fly. And the woods echoed with her joyous laughter, and the young Indian laughed as heartily as she did, apparently enjoying the triumph of her skill as much as he would his own in case he had killed the squirrel."

" Did they see you?" inquired the officer, with a heart almost ready to burst with rage and indignation at the young Indian.

" No; I was concealed in a bunch of bushes a short distance from them," replied Jo. "I wanted to see the sport and not disturb them with my presence. They appeared to me very much like lovers, although I don't know much about love myself, or how lovers ought to act."

" Did you see him kiss her?" asked Delano, almost breathless with anxiety.

" Certainly I did not," replied Jo. "He didn't make any attempt to kiss her, if he had, I suppose he might have done that thing, for he was near enough to her to take a kiss or give one."

" Were their faces near together?" asked the officer in a tremulous voice.

" Quite near when they were examining the hole the arrow had made in the poor squirrel's head," answered the imperturbable soldier.

" Then he didn't kiss her, you say?" replied Delano, feeling somewhat relieved from the sensations which crowded round his heart before Jo made his answer.

" Yes; I said he didn't kiss her; but then he might have kissed her," he answered. "They were so much engaged with the sport of shooting the squirrel that they put off the kissing business till some other time. No doubt the young fellow has kissed her a thousand times. What of that? Who could be alone in the woods with such red lips and not kiss them? Not I, if she would let me, and I hardly ever kissed a woman in my life."

" You do Lucelle injustice, sir," said the young officer, swelling with pride, but more with indignation against young Turok, for fear he had kissed the loved one of his heart.

" No injustice at all, lieutenant," replied the soldier, beginning to feel his temper rise a little at the pomposity manifested by Delano. "I have no doubt Lucelle is a virtuous female, and if she intends to marry that young Indian, there is no harm in permitting him to kiss her, or even in her kissing him."

" She never intends to marry him," answered Delano.

" Pray, sir, how do you know that?" asked the soldier in a stern manner.

" I had it yesterday from her own lips, and she would not speak falsely," said Delano.

" Very well, I will take her own declaration," replied Jo. "I didn't know as she had been questioned by any one in relation to that point; perhaps you have more interest in her than I was aware of. I yield the point, but at the same time I must be permitted to say that she will not marry any officer or soldier belonging to our establishment."

The soldier now began to be suspicious that Delano had been figuring round after Lucelle, and, if so, he was determined that she should know his true character and standing among the officers and soldiers of the garrison. Prideaux was well acquainted with him, and knew his origin and all about him. He suspected that Delano had been palming himself off upon her for a great deal more than he was; for he was considered the greatest liar and brágadacio there was in the whole camp. Jo Prideaux was a hard customer for the young officer, and it will be strange if he don't find him so.

" The officers of the fort will not call on you for a recommendation to the favour of any one, either man or woman," said Delano.

" I presume *some* of the officers will not," replied Prideaux, emphasising quite strongly the word some, "for, if they do, they would not be likely to gain much by it."

" Well, sir, you will please to attend to your duties while you're under my command, and give me no more of your saucy words," said Delano, very pompously.

Prideaux made no reply, except a contemptuous sneer upon his countenance might be construed into one. This intrepid soldier did not fear Delano, for there was not one in the company who would take sides with this young pompous officer; every one believed him to be a consummate scoundrel, and all knew he was an errant coward as ever wore an epaulette or dangled a sword.

The company now marched along, following the course of the brook, which flowed towards the south-east into the lake. Delano did not intend to go so far from the fort that he could not return to the fort before nightfall, for he was too much of a coward to be out after dark, and the soldiers knew it. As they slowly

marched along upon the banks of the brook, Prideaux hinted to his comrades that he would frighten their pompous leader before they proceeded much farther. It sometimes happened that Delano would pluck up courage, and walk ahead of his company, in order to show that courage which he did not possess; but more often he took his position at the side of the platoon, and strutted along there. Prideaux watched his opportunity, and, when Delano was marching along ahead of them, he sang out, in a voice that chilled the blood of the young man in his veins,—

No. 4.

"Hark! it seems to me I hear the tramp of the enemy."

All suddenly stopped, while Delano ran back, and placed himself as nearly in the centre of the company as he could in his fright and consternation

"Hark!" said another soldier, who understood the trick, in a voice scarcely above a whisper; "crouch down, and be still as death, or we may be fired upon, and our bodies made into riddling-siev s in the twinkling of an eye; for the British are sharp shooters."

The company immediately dropped on their knees to carry out the joke, and frighten their leader. The trembling and frightened Delano was not satisfied with kneeling, as the rest did, but he hugged the ground much closer than his companions did, and placed his head behind the posteriors of Prideaux, who had great difficulty in controlling himself, so as not to burst out into a fit of loud laughter. All remained in this position a few moments, apparently every instant expecting to hear the cracking of the enemy's guns.

"For God's sake let us retreat, and lose no time," whispered Delano, in a voice trembling with fear, close behind Prideaux. It seemed to Prideaux as if it were a voice from out of the ground, so close did the officer's face press the ground.

"For our country's sake, and for the glory of France, let us advance, and give our foes serious fight," said Prideaux, in a voice as resolute as he could make it for laughing, rising up, and aiming his gun, as if he were about to blaze away into the very hearts of their foes.

The whole company, following the example of Jo, rose up, and pointed their guns at the thick bushes ahead of them. Delano did not rise from his recumbent posture when the others did, but did soon after, and while their death-dealing weapons were levelled at the trees.

"Retreat—do not fire," exclaimed the trembling Delano, in the agony of his soul, turning on his heel, and retreating a few paces very rapidly. Finding the company did not obey his orders, but stood their ground firmly, with their guns at their shoulders, he stopped, and gazed upon them in the utmost anxiety. "Retreat," continued Delano, in a voice choked with fear, "and let us carry the report to the fort as soon as possible."

The company did not mind poor Delano, but, receiving a hint from Prideaux, they advanced slowly in the direction their guns were aiming, and were soon almost lost to the sight of their trembling leader, in the bushes. The young officer was now in a terrible quandary; he was afraid to advance, lest he should meet the enemy's fire; and he feared to retreat, lest he should be left alone; he stood trembling in that horrible dilemma, as if he would drop in pieces, and sink into the earth. Jo Prideaux always said, and stuck to it, that Delano's unmentionables were as wet as if they had been thrown into the brook, on the banks of which they stood; but whether this excess of moisture proceeded from profuse perspiration, or from some other cause, he left for others to judge; for he said he did not feel himself competent to settle that important question.

After the company had proceeded a short distance into the bushes, they halted and trailed arms. Delano saw this movement by some of those who were in the rear, and not out of his sight, and began to breathe more freely again; still he was almost petrified with fear. After the lapse of a few minutes, the company came back to the place where their valiant leader stood, with countenances unscored by battle, or distorted by fear.

"Have the enemy fled?" anxiously inquired Delano, staring wildly around him.

"I reckon they have," replied Prideaux, "for we couldn't see the whites of their eyes; if we had, you would have heard terrible cracking with our guns. We were determined to give them one broadside, and then, if they didn't retreat, to retreat ourselves, as fast as our legs would carry us."

"They may have gone round to cut off our retreat," said Delano. "We must be on march back to the fort; we are in danger every moment while we tarry here. Our orders were express that we must return immediately if we discovered the enemy, and bring the tidings to the fort."

"Well, have you seen him?" inquired Prideaux, struggling to repress a smile, which he felt rising from his heart to his lips.

"I have not, but I suppose you have," replied Delano.

"No, I haven't," answered Prideaux, looking very cunningly upon his commander.

"We haven't any of us seen the enemy with the naked eye, but yet he may be advancing, for all that," said another soldier, smiling most provokingly.

Delano was so much frightened, that he did not yet understand the trick they had played upon him, and was still trembling with fear. Notwithstanding the times were really critical, and the enemy was actually expected to besiege the fort of Ticonderoga, yet Prideaux and his companions enjoyed this sport with the young lieutenant with a right good relish.

"Let us retreat to the fort," said Delano. "Nothing will be gained standing here."

"But everything may be lost," replied Prideaux. "Hark? Didn't I hear something?"

The lieutenant again shook with fear, and even ran to the cunning Prideaux, as if that soldier could protect him from the assault of the foe he so much dreaded. Prideaux still kept himself in a listening attitude, very much to the amusement of his companions, as well as to the horror of their cowardly leader.

"After all, I believe I heard nothing but the water trickling over the pebbles," said Prideaux, smiling. "But it is well to keep a strict watch in these dangerous times. Better be over watchful than too careless and secure."

"I believe, now, we've all been frightened at our own shadows," said another soldier. "I think the enemy has not been near us. We had better proceed on and see what further discoveries we can make."

"No, we'll go no farther from the fort," said Delano. "We can take a circuit round, and so draw towards the garrison before nightfall. It will not be safe to be out after dark."

"Nonsense!" said Prideaux. "None but children are afraid of the dark. If the enemy approach us at all, they will do so by the way of Lake George. Our duty is to push on as far as the lake, and reconnoitre in that region. We can do so, and then return to the fort at a seasonable hour. If we should be out in the evening, the bears won't catch us. It is but a short distance to Lake George, and I move we go there before we return. It was expected that we should go as far as that at least."

Their cowardly leader remonstrated at first against such a proceeding, but finally yielded, with fear and trembling, to the general voice of the company. They now took a more westerly direction; but Delano was seen no more pompously strutting ahead of his company. He kept himself in the rear, greatly to the amusement of the whole party. They proceeded on, and soon stood on the shores of Lake George, a beautiful sheet of water, about thirty miles in extent. The scenery about this lake is grand and beautiful. For wildness and picturesque beauty it even exceeds that around Champlain. It was now approaching night, and discovering no signs of the enemy, they concluded it was best to start for Ticonderoga. None consented to this arrangement more readily and willingly than the young lieutenant. In going back to the fort, he even took the lead a part of the way, especially the last part. Neither Prideaux nor any of the rest of the company undeceived him as to the game they had practised upon him. True, he was not so much of a consummate fool as not to have any suspicions of them, for he did have, and could not well avoid it.

Soon after they left Lake George they heard a crackling noise in the bushes not far distant, and made a halt. Again the poor lieutenant was almost frightened to death. At first Prideaux and the other did not know but they might have come across a scouting party of the enemy, but soon their fears were quieted by the appearance of Turok. When he first came up to them, he was apparently much fatigued by hurried travelling in the woods; for big drops of sweat stood upon his manly brow and his finely chiselled nose dilated at every respiration.

The appearance of the young Indian indicated that he had made some important discoveries, and was on his way to inform the commander of the fort. All were glad to see him, with the exception of the lieutenant. He hated the looks of him now more than ever, since Prideaux had told of his trial of skill in shooting with his beloved Lucelle.

"Ah! well met," exclaimed Prideaux, as Turok emerged from the bushes and bent his steps towards him. "Some news of the enemy I dare say, for those big drops of sweat don't appear on your brow for nothing. 'Tis not a trifling affair which makes you sweat so."

Delano came up close to the young Indian with great anxiety depicted on his countenance, but Turok gave him a look of proud disdain, and retreated from him a few paces, as much as to say he did not wish to hold any correspondence with him. The lieutenant felt that his dignity was offended, and was highly displeased, but he concealed his ill-natured feelings as much as possible, and said, "Any news of the enemy? See any traces of them?"

Turok stood, and proudly and disdainfully gazed upon the young officer, but did not open his lips to make a reply. Prideaux and his companions were nighly gratified with this demonstration on the part of the young Indian; for if they ever despised any human creature, Delano was the being. Prideaux now thought he would see if he could not unloose Turok's tongue.

"You have seen some signs of the enemy, I know by your looks," said Prideaux. "You will tell me, an old friend and acquaintance, not only of yourself, but of somebody else, who resides at the other end of this brook. You understand, eh?"

A gleam of joy illuminated the manly face of the young Iroquois, while a dark shadow passed over the countenance of Delano, who ground his teeth together and clenched his hands in rage. Turok saw his anger, but he feared him not.

"I will speak to you of what I know of the enemy's movements, for you have too much courage to be frightened at your own shadow," replied Turok. "The enemy are approaching, and will besiege the fort in two or three days, and, perhaps, sooner."

"When did you see them?" anxiously inquired Delano.

"Be not alarmed, coward; for they are not within shooting distance yet," proudly replied Turok.

Prideaux and his companions could not refrain from laughing at the well-timed remarks of the young Iroquois. Poor Delano, but for his fear and cowardice, would have shown his wrath, and attempted to chastise the young savage for his insolence on the spot, but as it was, he grinned and bore the insult the best way he could.

"Then they won't fire upon us immediately," said Prideaux, laughing and winking at his companions.

"No, I think not," replied Turok, taking the hint and smiling most contemptuously upon Delano. "We can probably reach the fort with whole skins, unless some one of the company should die of fear, a horrible death for an officer or a soldier to die."

"True enough, Turok," replied Prideaux. "I should rather be shot any time than kick the bucket the way you speak of. I've no doubt some cowards actually suffer more pain in fearing death than they would if a bullet shot should go plump through them."

The young lieutenant felt as if he could almost swear to the truth of what Prideaux stated, although he had never had a bullet pass through him, and never intended to if he could avoid it.

"But where did you discover the enemy? inquired another soldier.

"Near the head of the lake," replied Turok "There appears to be quite an army of regulars and provincials encamped on the shores of the lakes, under the command of Gen. Amherst, as I was informed by an old Indian whose camp isn't more than half a mile this side of the enemy."

"Well, then, we shall have some warm work of it before we get through,"

Prideaux. "The British are determined to make no half way business of it this time. Do you think the enemy outnumber us ?"

"Three to one, I've no doubt," replied Turok. "The fort may hold out awhile against the siege, but in time would be obliged to surrender. The old Indian told me the British general had provisions and stores enough with him to prolong the siege until the fort would be starved out. The French, in my opinion, will have to yield sooner or later. If they make resistance and attempt to defend the fort, they will be taken prisoners of war, but if they abandon Ticonderoga and retreat to Crown Point, they may save themselves from such catastrophe."

"I'm of your opinion," said Prideaux. "But I should like the sport of making a few holes through the regulars with my trusty old piece."

"We will go to the fort immediately," said Delano. "Let us make no more delay. The information is important, and the sooner it is communicated to the commander of the fort the better it will be for all concerned."

"I will go on ahead and make the communication," said Turok. "Come, Prideaux, go with me. We can travel faster than the rest. The lieutenant might be fatigued should he attempt to keep up with us."

"I'll go with you," replied Prideaux, "if thy companions are willing."

They all readily gave their consent, but the intrepid leader. He was anxious to be the first one to deliver the message, but the young Iroquois was determined that Delano should not take any advantage to his own credit of the news he had been at so much pains to obtain. He preferred to be the bearer of the tidings himself.

"Nay, we will go together," said Delano. "It will have a more military appearance."

"Then I will go alone; for I'm not yet under your command, and probably never shall be," proudly replied Turok.

"And I'll go too," said Prideaux. "In times like these we mustn't wait for the orders of every little petty officer who thinks more of himself than other folks think of him."

And away ran Prideaux and the young Iroquois, leaving the lieutenant and his party to bring up the rear. In less than an hour, they reached the fort, and the important news was communicated to the commander. Great excitement now prevailed in the garrison. The commander of the fort had orders to retreat from place to place towards the centre of operations at Quebec, rather than to run the risk of diminishing the French force by surrendering prisoners of war. The young Iroquois was questioned in every variety of form. Some doubted the truth of the story he told, but the officers and soldiers generally believed his report, and governed themselves accordingly. At first the French appeared to be resolute to hold their works and make preparations for a regular defence—therefore immediately on the receipt of the intelligence which Turok brought, every man was engaged in doing something to strengthen the position which the French then held at Ticonderoga.

CHAPTER V.

It was a bright and beautiful morning the next day after the young Indian brought the intelligence to the fort of the movements of the enemy. Lucelle was out upon the lake in her canoe, taking a water excursion merely for her own pleasure. Much conversation had passed between her and her father relative to the interview they had with Lieutenant Delano, and the professions of love he had made, her father had become decidedly in favour of the pretensions of the officer to his daughter's hand. He had reflected much upon the proposals he had made. Dreams of again visiting Paris floated more than ever in his brain. He supposed his brother was still living and enjoying his ill-gotten estate. The height of his ambition was now to return to his native city under circumstances which might excite his brother's envy. Knowing he had a daughter whose beauty would vie with any in Paris, he felt ambitious to show her off in that proud metropolis. And now he vainly imagined he had an opportunity of exhibiting her as the wife of a gentleman of honour, fortune and fashion. These visions of splendour blinded his judgment, so that he could not see the true character of the man upon whom he so much relied to advance his favourite schemes. No; the father was much pleased with these bright prospects; and it may be quite naturally supposed that a portion of the same kind of spirit was breathed into the heart of the daughter. It was so: but yet Lucelle felt as if she could not love the officer, notwithstanding the dazzling prospects held out before her excited imagination by her union with him.

"Oh, how I long to be in Paris!" she said to herself, as she was peacefully resting in her light canoe upon the quiet bosom of the lake. "But yet I know I do not love Delano now. I wonder if I should love him. Father thinks I should love him after we were married and gone to Paris. But why should I be more likely to love him in the city than in the forest? Oh, I wish I knew. If Turok had as much money as Delano, and was not an Indian, I could be more happy with him. He loves me; but he never told me so. Delano is very bold in declaring his passion. After all he may not love me half so much as Turok does. Why do I dream so often of Turok! I wish I had never seen him, and then perhaps I might have loved Delano more. If I marry him, and go to Paris, I never shall see this beautiful lake I love so well, nor these hills and brooks, where I have roamed from earliest infancy. I'm not so happy now as I was a few days ago. It then seemed to me I should always live here, and have Turok for my friend and guide. It will be as hard to part from him as from these lovely scenes. I wish Turok would tell me how much he loves me. But why do I have such a wish? I cannot have an Indian for my husband. And why not? The same great Being made both races. No, no. I could not marry Turok, and yet my heart tells me I love him more than any other person, except my father."

While she was thus communing with her own thoughts, the young Iroquois saw her off on the lake, and went down to the landing. Seating himself on a rock, and fixing his eyes upon Lucelle, as she was floating over in the canoe he made with his own hands, he said within himself, "Oh, the Great Spirit has made me an Indian, and the proud heart of that yonder maiden will never let her marry me. Oh, that she knew how much I love her, and what sacrifices I would willingly make for her good. Does she know that I love her more than all things else on earth? I never told her with my lips, and yet my actions have been more eloquent than words. She must not marry Delano, for he's a villain and a coward. Prideaux has promised to tell me more about him, for he knows him well. He say he is not only a coward but a knave. Can Lucelle be pleased with him? Her father may, because he is an officer; but he's not fit for an officer, and all the soldiers say so. Ah! she's coming towards the shore. I will give her warning about Delano, and perhaps I may have courage to tell my own love for her. I wish I had done it months ago. But what good will it do? It will only trouble her, instead of affording her pleasure."

The fair nymph now turned the prow of her beautiful canoe towards the landing place, and, gracefully dipping her neatly carved paddle into the water, she soon ran her light vessel into the brook. She had not seen her Indian friend since she had parted with him at the same place some days before, when Delano was gazing upon him. As the canoe came up, he reached out his hand and politely waited upon her out of it—a thing he never did before in all his life.

"Good morning to you," she said, while a smile played over her flushed cheeks. "Where have you been?"

"To Lake George," he replied. "I came from there last night."

"Why did you go there?" she inquired. "Did you go hunting?"

"Not after such game as we usually kill at this season of the year," he replied.

"I went to see what discoveries I could make about the movements of the British. You know it h s been rumoured that they would attack the fort here, and I thought I would go and see if I could discover any traces of them."

'And did ou find out anything about them?" she inquired.

"Indeed I did," he answered. "There is a large army encamped on the shores of Lake George, and I have no doubt they will soon be here."

"Have you informed the commander of the fort?" she inquired.

"I have, and great preparations are being made to defend the fort against the attacks of the British," he answered. "But it will be in vain, for the British forces are too many for the French. The fort will be obliged to surrender, and the sooner it is done the better. If they do not abandon the works and fly to some other place, they will be all taken prisoners."

"I wish the French would conquer them," said Lucelle.

"So do I, but it is impossible," he replied. "How should you feel to have Lieutenant Delano taken prisoner and carried off?"

The fair nymph gazed upon him, and wondered why he should have made such a remark, for she did not suppose he could know anything of recent movements.

"You're silent, Lucelle, and look serious," he contin**** "Do you love Delano?"

"Oh, my friend, for such I must call you, I don't know what answer to make you," she replied. "Yes, I do, too. I can answer the simple question you asked me, and I will do so frankly. I must confess I do not love him: but father thinks he's rich, and we can all go to Paris."

"Go to Paris!" he repeated in a tone of voice which told how deeply he felt "Would you go to Paris and leave behind all these beautiful scenes—this lake, your canoe, these hills and trees, this little brook, whose wholesome waters you have drank so many summers, and above all, and more than all, the beautiful spot of earth which covers the earthly remains of your mother? Yes—can you, be willing to leave your mother's grave, which you have wet with so many tears, and the wild flowers growing upon it, which your own hands have watered so many times?"

Lucelle burst out into a flood of tears and wept like a child. Her heart was too full for utterance, and she sank down upon the rock, burying her face in her hands. The young and noble Iroquois bent over her, and the tears from his own eyes dropped upon her glossy silken hair. For some minutes both were silent, and too much overcome by the violence of their own emotions to break the silence and give vent to their feelings.

"I would not say aught to make you unhappy, Lucelle," he continued, in a voice full of sympathy and love. "But believe me when I say that I would do anything lawful to be done to make you happy."

"I know you would," she sobbed. "You are indeed my friend, and as such I esteem you as high as any one on earth. Perhaps I ought to except my father."

"Yes; your father is your best friend, now your mother rests in silence upon yonder hill-side; but I will make any sacrifice your father would for your happiness and comfort," he replied.

"Oh, Turok, we have spent many happy days together, and sometimes I wish they might never end," she answered in broken accents of grief and discomfort.

"Ah! Lucelle, indeed we have," he replied. "I too, wish they mght never end until death shall place you beside your mother in yonder grave. Would you be willing to have your body buried in a strange land so far away from your mother? I would not forsake the spot where my parents are buried for all the splendours which any city can afford. No, no, Lucelle. Let me die where I have lived, and the scene of death would be pleasant, when compared with dying in a distant and strange country."

The fair girl was agitated by powerful emotions. The voice of the young Indian was music to her ears, and she secretly wished Delano had such a voice.

"Do you love me ?" she asked, in a voice full of innocence and simplicity.

"Do you wish my lips to express what my actions have told you many a time ?" he replied. "Have they not spoken to you more eloquently than tongue can speak? Ah, yes, and more truly too, for the lips can easily lie."

"You need not tell me more," she said, in great agitation. "Why did I ask you such a question ? I did wrong, and hope you will pardon me."

"You've done no wrong," he replied. "You've never wronged any one, and cursed be he who accuses you of it. No, no, Lucelle. I've been in the wrong. I'm a dispised Indian. The white people look upon my race with contempt. I ought not to have loved you in the first place, and in the second I ought not to have told you of it. Long have I kept the secret closed up in my heart, except what my actions have revealed. You will pardon me for now disclosing it with my lips. I would have avoided it if I could, but at the moment I had no control over myself. You now know all. Despise me for it—forbid me to come into your presence—say you do not love me in return—anything—but do not place confidence in Delano, and leave the scenes of your youth and your mother's grave, to go with him into a distant and corrupt city. I fear he is a knave and will deceive you. He may pretend to love you, and perhaps he may now, but you never can be happy with him. His heart is corrupt, and yours is innocent. And how can two such hearts u   love ?"

"Do you know anything of his character?" she anxiously inquired. "Tell my father if you know him to be a villain. Better tell him than me."

"I know but little of him except what I have seen, but Joseph Prideaux has known him from his youth ; he can tell you and your father too all about him. He has promised to give me a history of him, but has not yet had time since I came from Lake George. Hush ! there he stands now, watching us as he did once before. I will leave you, and make him believe I did not discover him. Mark well what I have said, and be not deceived as you value your own happiness."

Saying this, he leaped across the brook, and with the fleetness of a deer bounded away among the trees of the forest. Lucelle had not time to bid him stay ere he was upon the margin of the brook, even if she had been disposed to lay such injunction upon him.

Soon as he had gone she started towards her father's lodge, but before she had proceeded far, Delano met her. She was much agitated, but concealed her emotions as well as she could under the pressure of circumstances which was then upon her.

"Oh, Lucelle, the British are expected here every day," he said. " I should have seen you last evening, but we were so busy in making preparations for defence against the expected attack of the British that I could hardly find time to breathe. There is great excitement in the fort. Many think we had better abandon the place rather than be taken prisoners by our enemies. I'm of that number."

"What does the commander think ?" she inquired.

"He hardly knows what to think," he replied. "He consulted me this very morning, and I gave him my opinion fully and frankly. If they insist upon fighting, I shall take leave myself, for I'm determined not to be taken prisoner, and carried the Lord only knows where. I'm unwilling to be forcibly separated from you now, when our prospects are so bright."

Lucelle made no reply to his remarks, for she was not very well pleased with such patriotism as he had shown. To leave the fort at such a perilous time, when it was necessary that every man should do his duty in order to defend it, did not look to her very officer-like nor patriotic. He thought it strange that she did not urge him to leave forthwith, and offer to conceal him in her father's lodge. This really looked equally strange to him, but he put the best face he could upon the matter, and let it pass without showing his spleen.

"I had a very fatiguing day yesterday," he continued. " I was despatched with a company of men on a reconnoitring expedition, and a set of more arrant cowards

I never knew. I ascertained at length that the enemy were encamped upon the shores of Lake George. Immediately I returned and gave the alarm to the officer of the fort."

Lucelle heard him through, and knew that either he, or Turok, had uttered a falsehood, but she was unwilling to believe for a single moment that her Indian lover was the guilty one ; for, during her whole acquaintance with him, and that had been ever since childhood, she had never known him to utter a single untruth. Upon everything he said she relied with the utmost confidence, and never doubted

his word. She thought she would not inform Delano of what Turok had told her, but let him go on without interruption on her part. Lucelle still remained silent.

"I saw that Indian bound away from you a few moments ago," he continued. " Why does he follow you round so much ? You ought not to condescend to speak with him, especially when you are alone with him, but instantly leave him unless he does you."

No. 5.

"Condescend to speak with him!" she repeated in surprise. "He is my friend and the friend of my father, and should I treat him like a dog?"

"No. You ought not to make so much of him as you would of a dog," he replied.

"Why, he has never injured me, nor insulted me, but on the contrary has done me and my father many favours," she answered, feeling her indignation rise at the cruel remarks he had uttered. "No, no, I must not, I cannot, I will not treat him thus. He was created by the same Being that created you and me, and I'm sure he is made in good form, and has a manly, honest countenance. I have never known him to utter a falsehood, and I don't think he would tell a lie on any consideration."

He started back suddenly, as if he had been pricked with some sharp instrument. Soon, however, he recovered his balance, and replied,—

"That may all be true, but then Heaven never designed that the Indians and whites should mingle together. If you suffer him to accompany you so much, it may soon be said that he is paying his addresses to you. This would be more than my proud spirit could bear. I have half a mind to chastise him for his impertinence in troubling you so much to keep out of his way."

"Oh, he don't trouble me at all," she innocently replied. "And if you should attempt the chastisement upon him you speak of, I fear you would be most severely beaten ; for he is a tremendous strong person. Father says he can flog any two men he has ever seen. I've seen him leap twice as far as across this brook. He can jump as far as a deer. I would not touch him if I were you."

"I could flog his eyes out in five minutes, if I should take hold of him in earnest," he replied, drawing himself up to his utmost height, and assuming a very courageous look. "Why, I whipped a man in the city of Paris who was twice as strong as Turok is. Ah, Lucelle, it would not be safe for him to fall into my hands. It is the generally received opinion, from some exhibitions of strength I have made, that there isn't a man in the fort I cannot handle as easy as the father corrects his child."

"I was not aware of your great strength," she replied. "You don't look so very strong."

"I may not, but my muscles are very firmly knit together," he answered, feeling the muscles of his arm, and placing her hand upon it.

"I will take your word for it," she said, in a very stern, reproving manner, suddenly withdrawing her hand, and gazing upon him most intently, as if she did not thank him for the liberties he had taken.

He was evidently displeased with her movement, but artfully concealed his irritated feelings, and requested her to go with him to the lodge, as he had but little time to spare, and wished to see her father. She consented, and they walked to the lodge, where they found the old hunter quietly smoking his pipe.

"Good morning, my good friend," said Delano to De la Motte, "I'm happy to see you thus enjoying yourself this fine morning, while we at the fort are all bustle and confusion. I hope one day to see you smoking a splendid pipe in your native city."

"I wish I were there now," replied the old man. "I begin to think I have lived long enough in the woods."

"Indeed you have, and I hope you will not be obliged to stay here much longer," replied Delano. "You've heard the news, I suppose, about the approach of the enemy?"

"Yes, Turok told me that he discovered the British encamped upon the shores of Lake George, and brought the news to the fort last night," replied the old hunter. "That young Indian is a smart fellow. A company like him would do essential service in keeping off the British."

Delano did not at all like the turn the conversation had taken. He was fearful that Lucelle might detect him in a falsehood, as her father had repeated what Turok told him, which did not square with his statement.

"My opinion is, that we must give up the fort, for we have not force enough to defend it against the numbers the British will bring into the field," said the officer. "I should be willing to fight as long as any man, but to fight against so much odds, and then be taken prisoners, is not true valour. Policy in war is my maxim. I might have been more willing to be taken prisoner, and carried away to Albány or Boston, if I had never seen your daughter, but now I cannot endure such a separation. It would be worse than death itself. If I found when fighting in defence of the fort, that I must be taken prisoner, I believe I should fight on until death put a final end to my action." He made this remark to see what effect it would have upon Lucelle. He was in hopes she would exclaim against such acts of temerity and rashness; but she remained most provokingly silent, and didn't seem to care whether he was killed or not.

"Then you think the French have not force enough to withstand the British?" said the old man. "That is my opinion, and I think they had better make good their retreat, when they can do so with safety."

"You're right in your conclusions," said Delano, rejoiced that the old hunter thought as he did upon this point. "If they still persist in fighting, I have thought I should leave them to their own destruction. I will not be taken prisoner so long as I have legs to make my escape. True courage does not require a man to stand and fight when he knows he shall either be shot or taken. If I should conclude to make my escape from the fort, couldn't I find a safe refuge in your lodge?"

Now this was Delano's object in visiting the old hunter, to ask a shelter from him, for he had trembled with fear ever since Joe Prideaux and others frightened him so yesterday. Besides, he was determined to have the old hunter's money, if he could not get his daughter, but both he would like to have the happiness of.

It was some time before the old man gave any reply. It was a subject upon which he deliberated very seriously before he made an answer.

"You hesitate," continued Delano. "It is for your daughter and yourself that I take this course. I want you to accompany me to Paris; but if I am taken prisoner, or shot in the heat or strife of battle, an end will be put to that project. My life I do not value but for the sake of Lucelle. I do not wish to live if I cannot have her to live with me. Without her, I count all my estate in Paris but dross, and with her I should prize every franc in proportion as it might add to her pleasure and happiness."

"I would do anything to save you from being taken prisoner, but the law is severe upon those who harbour deserters," said the old hunter. "I fear, if you should make my lodge your shelter, you would be found, and then both would have to suffer the severest penalty of the law."

"What, then, can I do?" anxiously inquired the lieutenant.

"Hide yourself in the woods till after the battle is over, and then join the victorious party," replied De la Motte.

"I'll do it," said Delano, jumping at the suggestion, and feeling as if he was now in a fair way to get rid of danger, which he so much feared.

"Be careful that you do not commit me in any way," said De la Motte. "Whisper nothing to mortal ears. Keep your own counsels, if you wish to have them safely kept, and trust them not to the keeping of any one."

"I will do so. I hope we shall meet again," said Delano, taking his leave and hurrying to the fort, for he had now been absent longer than he ought to have been.

"Father, do you think Turok would utter a falsehood?" inquired Lucelle.

"Why, Lucelle, do you ask such a question?" said her father. "Turok utter a falsehood? No; no man, woman, or child, ever heard him tell a lie. He would suffer his right hand to be cut off first."

"Then Delano has spoken falsely," she replied.

"How so?" he inquired, much surprised at Lucelle's declaration.

"Listen," she said. "Delano said he discovered the enemy, and brought the intelligence to the fort.   Turok told me he did.   Now there is a lie between them, and I'll never believe Turok has lied, unless I have strong proof."

" This must be looked into," said her father.   " If Delano will lie about one thing, he may about another, and no dependence can be placed upon him.   Joe Prideaux knows him.   I will ask him : he will tell me the truth."

" Turok says he's a coward and a knave, and I begin to think so," said Lucelle. " He also said that Prideaux could tell all about him, and warned me not to be deceived by him."

" I must confess, Lucelle, these circumstances excite my suspicions," he said.

" I'm satisfied, from what he has just said about deserting the army when his services are most needed, that he is a coward and a knave," replied Lucelle.   " I would never marry a man who would desert his country in a time of danger, if he were made of gold.   I could never be happy with him, if he treated me ever so well, because I should know his heart was corrupt.   I'm really afraid of him."

The old hunter's suspicions, as well as his daughter's, were excited, and he was determined to probe the matter to the bottom.

CHAPTER VI.

ANOTHER day had passed, and the enemy had not made his appearance before the fort.   The note of preparation was still heard among the French, and the young Iroquois was scouring the woods in every direction in the vicinity of the garrison, and watching the movements of the British.   No one was more anxious than he was to have the French come off victorious, and yet his hopes were by no means buoyant.   From what he saw of the enemy, and from what the old Indian told him, he was forced to believe that the British regulars and provincials would have an easy task to drive the French from Ticonderoga.

Lucelle too was as anxious as young Turok.   Often might she have been seen taking a circuit of more than two miles from the fort, and looking out for the approach of the enemy.   She was not afraid of being captured or killed by the British.   Her father tried to keep her in his lodge, but ever since Turok had informed her the enemy were encamped at Lake George, she was exceedingly anxious to do something for the good of the French.   All her partialities were in their favour, and her prejudices against the English.   It was an interesting sight to see this beautiful nymph racing through the woods with the fleetness of the deer, her long, dark hair flowing over her neck and shoulders, and her eyes sparkling with the brilliancy of the gazelle's.

Joe Prideaux, at the head of the six soldiers, was despatched to watch the first approach of the enemy, and a better soldier could not have been selected from the garrison.   Bold, resolute, and yet cautious and shrewd, he was ever present where duty called him.   He had six good trusty Frenchmen with him, who were ready to fight at any moment.   Prideaux kept constantly in motion, determined that the enemy should not approach unless he discovered him in season to give timely notice to the commander of the fort.   The part of the forest where he kept his vigils most was some two or three miles from the fort to Lake George on the route he supposed the enemy would not usually take.   He knew the ground so well that he had no doubt Amherst with his army would pass not far distant of the place he had selected as the theatre of his operations.

" Hark !" whispered Prideaux to his men as they stood beside a crystal spring which gushed out from under a large rock, on the side of a small hill, distant from the fort nearly two annd a half miles, " I thought I heard footsteps of man or beast.   Yes—don't you hear the bushes crackle?"

Soon as the words had escaped the soldier's lips, Lucelle emerged from some thick alders which grew in a small valley through which the water from the spring ran. She wore a light cap of blue cloth and a calico loose dress, bound round her waist with a narrow strip of tanned deer skin, and moccasins upon her small feet, made from the same material. The dress came down about half way between her knees and ancles, disclosing a pair of finely moulded legs as ever any French *danseuse* sported on the stage. Her moccasins were made by Turok's mother, and after her decease, he gave them to Lucelle. She had on, also, leggings or pantalettes, made of deer skin, elegantly wrought with moose hair, and neatly fitted to her leg. These were also a present from an old Indian squaw who was a great friend to her father for the kindness he had shown her husband when in distress. She had a small gun upon her shoulder, and a feather from the wing of an eagle in her cap. She had purposely rigged herself out in this style, thinking she might meet the enemy, and if she did, she wished to look as handsome as she could, and excite their admiration. Her pantalettes and moccasins she did not wear often, but she put them on now for the purpose of adding to her beauty.

"Ah ! it is neither man nor beast," continued Prideaux, as Lucelle, with light step and graceful motion, approached them. "It is Lucelle de la Motte, armed and equipped as the law directs. She is a beautiful creature, and will shoot more hearts with her dark eyes, than bodies with her gun."

With a smile on her beautiful face, she ran up to the spring, and taking a little birch bark cup from her girdle, dipped it into the cool waters and drank.

"I was very thirsty," she said, "I know this little spring well, and have drunk of its pure water many a time. Will you have my cup and drink also, or have you already slaked your thirst ?"

"We have drunk once, but we'll drink again for the sake of drinking from your beautiful dish," replied Prideaux, taking the cup and dipping into the spring.

"This water is really refreshing to us soldiers," she said, smiling and drawing her symmetrical form up in true miltary style.

"True, Lucelle, and we'll drink to the glory of France," said Prideaux, drinking himself, and handing the little cup to Lucelle, who drank and gave it to the others. "I think I can tell who made this cup and gave it to thee," continued Prideaux, smiling.

"You may try," she replied, and almost charming the company with her bright, sparkling eyes.

"The young Iroquois," replied Prideaux, winking very significantly. "It is a perfect specimen of his ingenuity. He's a glorious fellow, Lucelle, and you need not be ashamed to own him as a friend."

"Indeed I am not," she replied. "You have guessed right. He did make it, and gave it to me some months ago."

"I thought so," he replied. "There is a certain finish about everything he touches his hand to, which I always know. He's the best fellow we have. It was he who first discovered the enemy and brought intelligence to the fort."

"I thought it was Lieutenant Delano," she replied, wishing to learn something of his character. "He told me he did, and surely a French officer would not lie, would he ?"

"Delano !" repeated Prideaux, bursting into a loud laugh, joined by all the others, who knew him as well as Prideaux did. "Delano ! Lieutenant Delano !" repeating over the name, and laughing still more loudly.

The loud laughing of Prideaux and his company spoke more eloquently to Lucelle than any words they could have uttered. From it she learnt their opinion of the young lieutenant without doubt.

"Then you know the young officer, do you ?" she inquired.

"Yes, like a book,' replied Prideaux. He's a most arrant coward, besides being a consummate knave. I frightened him most prodigiously in the woods, the day Turok discovered the enemy. We had sport enough with him for one day. He trembled like a poplar leaf. At one time I thought the spasms wouldcarry him off to the other world."

"Is the city of Paris his native place?" asked Lucelle.

"No, he was born in a log house in Cape Breton," he replied; "but then he's none the worse for having been born in a cot, if he did not attempt to make folks believe that he sprung from noble origin in France. His parents are poor as church mice; but then he's none the worse for that, if he didn't attempt to force the belief upon people that they were rich, and that he has a great estate in France. Ah! Lucelle, he's a miserable dog, make the most of him you can. Be not deceived by him. His vanity I could endure but for his corrupt heart. That would carry him any length in crime. All the restraining grace he has about him is his cowardice. This may prevent him from committing any flagrant crimes, where courage is required in their commission. Be on your guard against him, and trust him not."

"Why was he not sent out to-day on a reconnoitring excursion?" she inquired.

"There are two very good reasons for that," replied the soldier. "In the first place he's no more fit for it than a monkey; in fact I should prefer a decent sized baboon; and in the second place he can't be found. He's among the missing; he ran away yesterday, very much to the gratification of the officers and soldiers of the fort. If he should be found, they might and probably would, take notice enough of him to shoot him."

"I thank you for your frankness in telling me just what I wanted to know," she said. "He has been telling his pompous stories to my father, and he was more than half inclined to believe them."

"Luckily for you, Lucelle, that you have learnt the coward's true character." said Prideaux; "but he has cleared out, and fortunate will it be for him if he is not discovered."

"Will he not return, think you?" she inquired, concealing what she knew about his designs to desert the French army, and his asking to be sheltered in her father's lodge.

"Not so long as the sound of a gun is heard, or the gleaming of a sword is to be seen," replied the soldier. "I should not be at all surprised to hear that he had joined the enemies of his country, should they happen to be victorious."

Lucelle recollected that her father had told him to join the victorious army, and she regretted the circumstance most bitterly, but she had too much shrewdness and cunning to reveal the fact to Prideaux and his companions in arms, well knowing that such advice, coming from her father, might cost him his head. She had often urged him to lend his aid to the French, in their struggles for liberty against the British, but he had always refused, and would take no part in the wars upon either side. The English he never liked, and the French government, once having rejected his petition for a pardon, he never would forgive the injury, and invariably refused to take up arms in defence of the rights of the colonies.

"Do you expect the enemy will attack the fort soon?" she inquired.

"Every hour I'm expecting to discover some advance guards, or reconnoitring parties, sent out by General Amherst," replied the soldier. "The British general is a cautious, prudent officer, I'm informed, and we must look out for his wily movements."

"Do you intend to shoot some of the red-coats?" asked Prideaux. "You're armed, I perceive."

"Oh, no; father has forbidden me to fire a gun on either side, but I thought I would come out, and see if I could make any discoveries, and inform the officers of the garrison."

"Well done, brave Lucelle," said Prideaux; "I like your courage. Come, will you go with us? It is time we were on the move."

"I will go alone in another direction, and, if I see any movement of the enemy, I will fly to the fort with the fleetness of the deer," she replied, while her eyes sparkled with great brilliancy, and her bosom swelled with patriotic emotions.

"The British regulars couldn't catch me—I'm more accustomed to running through these forests than they are."

Prideaux and his companions laughed heartily at Lucelle's courage, and, praising her for her good qualities, wheeled off from the spring, and struck into the woods towards Lake George, leaving the fair goddess of the forest to take her own course. Having taken another cooling draught from the spring, she started off towards the south. She pursued that direction some time without making any discoveries. While she was thus wandering about, young Turok was reconnoitering in another direction. As he passed along through some thick bushes that grew on a low piece of ground, in his way towards Lake George, further south than Prideaux and his party directed their course, he heard a rustling among the fallen leaves, and crackling of some dry sticks. He suddenly stopped and listened, but all was still. The sounds which struck his ears a moment before were now hushed, and nothing was heard but the purling of a little brook, which ran through the valley near where he stood. He observed the direction from which the sounds proceeded, and bent his steps cautiously towards the place, his gun cocked, and half raised to his shoulder, ready for any emergency.

Lieutenant Delano (for it was he whom the young Indian heard) had a faint glimpse of the form of a man through the bushes, and, supposing it to be one of the men from the fort, he softly crept under a windfall, and concealed himself in the dry tap, stowing his body as closely as he could under the trunk of the fallen tree, which was borne up a short distance from the ground by the limbs. The poor officer lay in this place of concealment still as he could; but he was so much frightened, that his hard breathing fell on the quick ear of the young savage, and led him to the spot where the coward had so snugly bestowed himself.

"Come forth !" said Turok, in a clear, distinct voice, as he stood upon the trunk of the fallen tree, but a few paces from the trembling deserter.

Delano knew the voice of the young Iroquois, and he trembled a thousand times more than if a British soldier had stood before him. The cowardly deserter was then on his way to join his enemies, and give them all the information in his possession ; but Turok did not know this fact, neither did he suspect it, for he thought Delano was even too much of a coward for that. The deserter kept his position, and did not at first obey the summons of the Indian.

"Come forth, you coward, or I'll leave your carcass for the eagle and the crow to feed upon," continued Turok, drawing his gun to his shoulder, and pointing it at the trembling lieutenant.

Delano saw the gun aiming at him, and expected every moment to hear the sharp report, and feel the bullet pierce his heart. Unable to hold still any longer, he sprang from his hiding-place and attempted to run, but the young Indian was too quick for him, for before he was ten feet from the place of his concealment, Turok bounded towards him like a tiger, and seized him by the shoulder. Delano trembled under his grasp, as if an catamount was upon him.

"Let me go, and I will never be seen in these forests again," exclaimed Delano, in a voice choked with cowardly fear. "Do let me go, and I will fly from these regions."

"Whither would you flee?" asked Turok, tightening his grasp upon the officer's shoulder and gazing into his fear-stricken countenance.

"Anywhere you may please to order," replied Delano.

"Would it not be safer to carry you back to the fort, and there let you be shot as a deserter?" asked Turok, in a voice which made his victim tremble in every joint and muscle.

"Oh, for Heaven's sake, do not carry me back to the fort," he exclaimed, so piteously, that the Indian's sympathy was really excited. He thought he never heard such a mournful cry from human throat before.

"Would you deceive a fair young nymph, and pass yourself off for some great man?" inquired Turok. "Villain ! Wretch !" You deserve death."

"Oh, spare me," he exclaimed in a tone of voice which would have penetrated a heart of stone. "I will not attempt to deceive her, I will leave the country, go anywhere, do anything, if you will but release me. I will give you my sword and my watch, and they are valuable ones."

" Will you promise to leave the country and never be seen in it again, if I will release my grasp and let you go," said Turok.

" I will promise—I swear by——"

" Stay," said Turok. " Do not swear, lest you might be tempted to perjure your own soul. I ask you not to swear, for he who would not keep his promise without an oath would not with one. Your swearing would have no effect on me. The white man takes too many oaths and too lightly esteems them. No, no. I will not hear you swear; and although you deserve death, I will not be your executioner."

" You will let me go, then? Here, take my gold watch and my sword," he said, taking his watch from his pocket and presenting it to him, together with his sword.

" I will not take your watch, for that you may need in your journeyings ; but your sword I will keep, for that you are too much of a coward to use, even in self-defence," Turok replied, receiving the deserter's sword.

" Thanks ! a thousand thanks !" exclaimed Delano.

" I ask not your thanks," replied the young Indian. " Reserve them for others, who may believe in their sincerity. Go, and never let me see you again, or I may be tempted to take your miserable life. That temptation I wish to avoid. Go, and leave the country, lest others who may be more cruel than I am should bring you to justice, and your life pay the forfeit of your crimes."

" I will leave the country, and never more be seen here," he said, bounding away from the young Indian, and leaving his sword in his possession.

" He's gone, and I hope for ever," soliliquised the noble son of the forest. " He may join the enemy and seek protection from them. But if I ever see him lurking around her again, I may be tempted to shed his blood. Lucelle could never have loved him, and yet she might by his dazzling, deceitful stories, and her father's influence, have been induced to marry him. But loving her as I do, I had much rather see her fair form floating a corpse upon the waves of yonder lake than witness her marriage to such a man. It must never be ! It shall never be ! No power on earth can effect such an unholy, unnatural alliance as that would be. The great Spirit would not approve of it. I'll watch for him, and protect the innocent and beautiful maid from such a curse. If she will not marry me, she shall not wed such a scoundrel as Delano."

Thus communed this gallant son of the forest as he pursued his way in search of the enemy's movements. Delano, after he had got clear of Turok, wandered about in the woods, and knew not what course to pursue. When Turok found him, he was on his way to find the British army, and turn traitor to his own country, but his arrest by the Indian had somewhat frustrated his plans, and changed his purposes. Having proceeded nearly a mile, and feeling in some measure secure from the vengeance of Turok, he sat down upon a rock and seriously reflected upon his situation. He thought, if he did not join the British army, he might be taken by his own party and shot as a deserter, and if he did join it, and it should not win the battle, he very well knew he should be in a worse situation. For some time he debated the question most seriously, starting at the sound every squirrel made in passing near him, and frightened at the noise of every bird's wing that he heard over his head. He was in a sad quandary, and knew not which way to turn. Sometimes he thought he would go back to the fort, and ask for pardon ; but this was not only a humiliating, but a dangerous course, for he was not sure of being forgiven if he did go back. After much reflection, he came to the conclusion that the safer course for him to take would be to join the British, fully believing that they would gladly receive him ; he therefore rose from the rock, and bent his steps towards Lake George, where he supposed the English army was encamped. Not being troubled with a sword to dangle about his legs, or become entangled in the bushes, he made good speed and progress on his route.

Having travelled as fast as his legs would carry him, about three-fourths of a mile in the direction which he supposed would lead him to the British encampment, he heard a noise ahead of him as if some one was travelling in great haste. He was much frightened, but before he could conceal himself under another tree-top, the fair Lucelle met him face to face. She instantly cocked her gun, and brought it to her shoulder as if she were about to fire.

"Hold ! dear Lucelle," he exclaimed, dropping upon his knees in terrible fear, and gazing wildly into her face. "Don't fire ! It is I—your own friend and lover."

"Own friend and lover !" she repeated, recognising who he was that knelt so humbly before her. When she first met him, she did not know him, but thought he might be one of the enemy lurking about.

"Yes, one that adores you," he replied, "and would lay down his life to save yours. You didn't recognise me at first, did you ?"

No. 6.

"No, I did not, and would to Heaven I had not now," she replied, her dark eyes flashing fire, and her heart beating with strange emotions. "Friend and lover indeed!" she continued. "Coward and traitor! Say that, and for once in your life you will speak the truth."

"Why don't you know me?" he asked, still on his knees before her. "I am Lieutenant Delano, he who loves you most dearly."

"Yes; I know you but too well," she sternly replied. "Prideaux has given me a history of your character. You are not only a most arrant coward, but also a most hypocritical scoundrel and consummate knave. Rise from your knees, and humbly bend yourself before Him whose pardon and forgiveness may save you from a dreadful punishment. Get out of my way, for I have important news for the fort, and I must hence and carry it."

"What news, pray, dear Lucelle?" he anxiously inquired. "Have you discovered the British?"

"Yes, there's a party of them not more than two miles distant on their march towards the fort," she replied,—"Go and join them—turn traitor to your country —shoot your friends, if you have courage to fire a gun—do anything—no crime can make your black heart any more corrupt than it is now."

And she bounded away, and left the agitated lieutenant still bending upon his knees. The fair nymph flew through the woods with the speed of a bird, and delivered her important message to the commander of the fort. She had disco-vered a party of the British cautiously marching through the forest, some distance in advance of the main army. This reconnoitring company was under the com-mand of Col. Roger Townshend, a young British nobleman of great merit, distin-guished ability, and much personal beauty. It was said he much resembled Lord Howe in the circumstances of birth, age, character, and useful qualifications.

When Lucelle arrived at the fort, it was about the middle of the afternoon; the intelligence which she brought added much to the excitement which already existed in the fort. All hands were now engaged in placing the guns upon the batteries, and preparing to give the enemy a warm reception. Although many and perhaps a majority of those in command, and the soldiers too, were for abandoning the fort, and retreating down the lake to Crown Point, yet no definite arrangements had been made for such a movement, and therefore they placed them-selves in the best attitude of defence they could. Perhaps they would have been better prepared, if they had been more united in council and opinion, but as it was, they were in a poor condition to make a good defence of their works.

Soon after Lucelle arrived with the intelligence of the enemy's movements, Turok came to the fort all covered with sweat, bearing the same news. He ex-pected to be the first to give the information but when he learnt that Lucelle had been the first carrier, he could not help feeling a secret delight that it was she in-stead of Prideaux or any one else, that had shorn him of the honour of being the first to discover the enemy, and bring the tidings to the garrison.

After Lucelle had delivered her message, she hastened to her father to inform him of the discoveries she had made, touching the movements of the enemy, but more especially to disclose to him the facts she had learnt from Prideaux in rela-tion to Delano. She told him all Prideaux had related to her, and gave him a very descriptive account of her last interview with the once pompous, but now humble lieutenant. The old hunter shook his head, and expressed his fears to her that Delano was exasperated, and maddened as he must be, might find oppor-tunity to wreak his vengeance upon them. But Lucelle told him Delano was too much of a coward to attempt any violence. She also took encouragement from the fact that the young Iroquois was a friend and would guard them from all harm. Her father thought Lucelle grew more and more in favour of Turok every hour, especially since she had found out the true character of Delano. He had always supposed that her natural pride would prove an impassible barrier to her marriage with the young Iroquois, but recently he entertained some doubts and misgivings upon the point. His own pride was such that his consent could never be obtained to the marriage of Lucelle with an Indian. He was fully determined that such an event should never take place in his lifetime. And he began to erect barriers against such a consummation, and to lecture her seriously upon the subject.

CHAPTER VII.

AFTER Delano had his interview with Lucelle in the woods, and she had informed him that a British reconnoitring company were on the march towards the fort, he hastened with all speed to find them, and to throw himself on their protection. In a short time after Lucelle bounded away from bearing the tidings to the commander of the garrison, he discovered Col. Townshend and his company, taking some refreshment upon the margin of a small brook, which came down from a mountain distant about a mile from them, and ran into the lake south of the fort which they were about to reconnoitre. The gallant young colonel did not know exactly which way to direct his course, and was debating the question when Delano made his appearance. Townshend was the first to discover the French lieutenant, as he was very cautiously coming towards them, making all the signs in his power of his friendship.

"Ready!" exclaimed the colonel the moment his eyes fell on poor Delano.

"The enemy is approaching. Every man to his duty, and we'll soon disperse the French cowards."

The instant the order was given, in a clear distinct tone of voice, for which the young officer was remarkable, every gun was brought to the shoulder, as if it had been done by magic or some kind of machinery.

"Wait for the word," continued the commander. "But one has made his appearance yet, and we won't waste powder and ball upon him, for he seems to be unarmed."

"Don't fire! for God's sake don't fire!" exclaimed Delano, almost frightened out of his senses, and reeling about as if he were drunk. "I'm alone, and your friend. Protect me, and I will tell you all I know."

"That won't take him long, unless his looks belie him," said one of the soldiers.

"I believe he's a drunken French officer," said Col. Townshend. "Perhaps we can get something out of him which will be of service."

"A tight squeeze for that," said the soldier aforesaid. "He hasn't much in him but French brandy, and that would make a dog sick."

"I'm not in liquor," said Delano, in a voice tremulous with fear.

"But liquor is in you, though," replied the waggish soldier.

"Come, Readman, you're always joking," said Colonel Townshend. "I believe you would crack a joke even while the French guns were cracking at you. There's no time now for mirth. We'll have that when we're in possession of Ticonderoga, and I trust that will be before to-morrow's sun goes down."

"You can take it quite easily," said Delano, approaching the colonel and reaching out his hand in token of friendship.

"Stand back at a proper distance," said the cautious colonel. "I know not but you may have some deadly weapon in one hand, while you extend the other in token of a friendship you do not feel. I will hear your story before I hug you too closely."

"No danger from his embrace, unless he's got the itch or is lousy," said the soldier.

The colonel could not restrain himself from laughing, and neither could the soldier.

Delano looked as if he hadn't a friend in the world. His lips quivered, his eyes rolled wildly about in their sockets, his hands trembled, and his knees smote one against the other. He was indeed an object of pity as well as of laughter. How different was his appearance now from what he assumed when he was pompously telling old De la Motte and his daughter of his estate in Paris, and the splendour to which he desired to lead the beautiful Lucelle? How fallen was the lieutenant ! He was now a suppliant at the feet of the British soldiery, whose power he once so proudly defied.

"I have no weapon—no disease—I'm a deserter from the French at the fort," said Delano. "I will fight on your side if you will protect me."

"You shall fare as well as we do," said the colonel. "You're come just in time, for we need a pilot to direct us the nearest and best way to the enemy's fort. British guns shall protect you so long as you fight under England's standard."

Delano did not like the idea of going back to the fort with so small a company. He was fearful, if he accompanied them, that he might be taken by those whom he had deserted, and shot for his treason. He was anxious to be with the main army, for in that he thought he might find protection and safety: but to go with this small company made his nerves tremble.

"Where is the main army of the British?" inquired Delano.

"They are but a short distance behind, some three or four miles," replied the colonel. "We are going on to reconnoitre the French works, see how strong their fortifications are, and give them a few guns as an earnest of what we intend to do. The main body of soldiers will not advance till morning, when we expect to give the French a pretty hot breakfast, unless they surrender peaceably."

"We shall make the rocks and gravel fly about their heads right merrily in the morning," said the waggish soldier. "And before we sleep, we intend to let them hear some thunder. Do you think they will stand fire boldly?"

"I would not go this afternoon," said Delano. "They are more numerous than we are, and we shall be taken. Let us go back to the army and all go together in the morning."

"Gen. Amherst is too cautious and shrewd an officer to risk an engagement until he has used all means within his power to ascertain the position of the enemy and his strength," replied Colonel Townshend.

"Yes—that's the way we do up our business," said the soldier. "We mean to stick our fingers in the fire and see how hot it is before we run our heads into it."

"We shall all be shot, for they have large guns mounted upon the breast works, all charged, and ready to be touched off at a moment's warning," said the French lieutenant, looking imploringly in the gallant colonel's face, and trembling as if he would shake into a thousand pieces.

"We must go so near them before nightfall that we can see the whites of their eyes," said the soldier, intending to frighten poor Delano, and make sport for his comrades.

"Then we shall certainly all be killed," replied Delano, sitting down upon a rock which was near him, and quaking with fear.

"We must obey orders and proceed to the fort forthwith," said the colonel. "The ground must be surveyed and the best mode of attack hit upon before the main army comes up. We are fortunate in having a pilot who can show us the lay of the land and the best mode of attack."

"Let me go to the main army, and I will draw a plan of the fort to-night, and tell Gen. Amherst how to proceed in the morning," said Delano. "This will be decidedly the best course and the wisest policy."

A smile passed over the manly face of Col. Townshend, in spite of all his efforts to restrain it; and the soldiers came near bursting out into an immoderate fit of laughter at the appearance of the trembling Frenchman, as he sat upon the rock before them. His looks pleaded more eloquently than any words he could utter. Colonel Townshend really pitied him, but still he felt it his duty not to let the deserter escape, for he did not know but he might be a spy, and instead of going to Gen. Amherst, bend his steps in some other direction. It is true Delano had every appearance of being what he represented himself to be, and the colonel had but few doubts upon the point, still duty compelled him to take the trembling deserter along with him, however reluctant he might be to accompany him.

"You must go with us," said the colonel. "You have thrown yourself upon our protection, and we cannot let you pass. We will take as good care of you as we do of ourselves. We will not ask you to go into any danger we are not willing to meet ourselves. Show us the way, and we will go forward, and you shall bring up in the rear. We've no more time for words. Action is our motto."

Reluctant as Delano was, he had to obey orders, and marched on towards the fort. It was fun to the soldiers to see the poor lieutenant suddenly start at every noise he heard, which he imagined did not proceed from the company whose pilot he was. Colonel Townshend gave him strict orders to be faithful and pilot them according to his best skill and judgment, impressing upon him the fear that immediate death would be his portion the moment he proved a traitor to them.

The sun was about an hour and a half high when they came within sight of the fort. The colonel went upon a elevated piece of ground not more than eighty rods from the fortifications, and with the aid of his glass he could see how they were situated. As Delano had told him, cannons were placed upon the breastworks, and men were distinctly seen standing by them as if they were momentarily expecting an attack. He descended from the small hill where he stood and gave orders to his men to proceed towards the fort. They had not proceeded far, before they heard the report of a gun and a bullet whistling over their heads. It struck a tree not far from Delano. He fell to the ground almost as suddenly as if the bullet had pierced his heart. Col. Townshend ordered his men to advance while he ran to see if Delano was really wounded or not, but he found him unscarred except by fear. He told him to rise and follow on, or he would be left alone. This so much alarmed the lieutenant that he rose and followed tremblingly along.

"There are too many for us, and we will retreat to the fort," said Joseph Prideaux to his six men, who were out as a sort of picket guard. "I'll give them the contents of my piece, and show them that we are alive and well. Reserve your fire till we reach the fort. It will be needed there."

Prideaux fired, and this was the report which so much alarmed Delano. Prideaux and his men then retreated to the fort. Colonel Townshend pressed on in pursuit of Prideaux and his comrades, but he could not get near enough to give them a shot before they entrenched themselves behind the breastworks. Townshend pressed on until he found he was quite near enough to the enemy's cannon for safety. Great alarm was felt within the fort, for the French could not ascertain how large the force was which Townshend brought up. While they were standing and examining the fortifications and positions of the French, Townshend's eye fell on Lucelle de la Motte, who hastened back to the fort after she had related to her father what Prideaux had told her concerning Delano. She did not go into the fort, but was round in the vicinity of it, watching all the movements.

"Ah!" said Townshend, "there is a beautiful female with a feather in her cap and a gun upon her shoulder. She seems to be looking at us, but we will not fire at her unless she makes some hostile movements. She's a splendid creature!"

The young and gallant colonel was so much interested in her, that he took out his glass to scan her person more closely.

"She is, indeed, a most beautiful girl, straight as an arrow, and raven locks all over her shoulders," continued the colonel, examining her through his glass. "She's not an Indian, although she's dressed somewhat like one. Now she moves, and how gracefully she walks."

"It is Lucelle de la Motte," whispered Delano, in extreme agitation "Don't let her see me. She will inform the whole garrison, and I shall be shot."

"Who the devil is Lucelle de la Motte?" asked the humorous soldier, "Let her come here, and if she's as pretty as the colonel says she is, I should rather kiss her twice than shoot her once."

"She's the daughter of an old hunter, who lives a short distance beyond the fort, down by the lake," replied Delano. "Don't let her see me. There! She's gone out of sight. She'll inform the commander of the fort that we are here."

"He knows that already," said Townshend. "Let her go. She can do us no harm now, and she's too beautiful to fire a gun."

While they were thus conversing, Lucelle passed from their view, and went towards the lake. Her beauty of face and form, and her graceful motions, made quite an impression upon the young and accomplished colonel. He thought he had never seen such a beautiful female in his life, among all the women in whose society he had mingled, and these were by no means a few, for he had been a most successful gallant among the ladies, and highly esteemed by them for his courtly manners and his manly beauty. But few young noblemen of England were more highly accomplished than Colonel Roger Townshend. He was beloved by the soldiers, and General Amherst considered him his right hand man in this expedition against the French colonists.

The colonel and his men now cautiously proceeded nearer the fort, but still he thought he was beyond the reach of the enemy's big guns. While he was thus slowly and cautiously advancing, Prideaux was upon the breastwork beside the largest gun in the fort, watching, with eagle eyes, the movements of Townshend, and determined to give him a shot if he came within anything like reasonable distance.

"Be ready with your match," said Prideaux, addressing Turok, who stood beside him, ready to touch off the gun when the word was given. "They advance—we may have a chance to reach them yet. The leader is a bold fellow—he walks proudly up—he's an Englishman all over. I'll give her old muzzle the right direction, and you touch her off the instant I give the word."

Prideaux stood at the breech of the gun, looking along its rusty back and moving it so as to get a fair aim.

"Are they not near enough now?" anxiously inquired the young Iroquois. "It seems to me I could almost reach them with my gun."

"Not quite yet," replied Prideaux, "They still advance. There! they have made a halt—they'll not come nearer. Ready! Fire!"

The report of the gun went echoing through the valleys, and booming over the lake like a heavy peal of thunder. Lucelle was near the lake shore when Turok touched his match to the cannon. The deafening sound struck upon her ear, and she started as if the ball had struck her. She hurried up the bank to see the fight, but when she ascended upon the high ground all was still. No sounds of guns, nor clanging of swords, was heard.

"Not but one gun?" she said to herself, as she stood upon a high bluff, which commanded a full view of the fort and all its breastworks. "I thought there would be a battle. Has the enemy retreated? Will the sound of a single French gun frighten the British? That gallant young man who led on his company did not look as if fear would make him retreat. He was a noble-looking officer, and how sharply he gazed upon me through his glass! All is still—I'll go nearer the fort and see what the movement is."

"Ah! they fly, and the best-looking one has fallen," said Prideaux, as soon as Turok had applied the match to the gun. "I thought we should fetch him. He struggles, and may not be mortally wounded! It is their leader, and they have fled like frightened deer. I reckon they feared a second charge."

"I've a mind to go and see what we've done," said Turok; "it gives me pain to see him struggle so, and raise his hands for help. Why did his cowardly comrades run and leave him in such an extremity?"

"No, no—you mustn't go yet," replied Prideaux. "They may be concealed in the bushes, and while you were examining the wounded man, they might make a riddling sieve of your body. Let us wait until we're sure they have retreated.

It was a bold move to come up so near. But, I suppose, they thought French guns couldn't reach so far. Ah! he lives yet and may recover. Let us charge again and give him a second potion."

"Nay!" said the young Indian, "I will not fire at a wounded man when all his comrades have abandoned him. I will go and see him."

"Hush! there comes one towards him," said Prideaux, "and a woman, too, I believe."

"It is Lucelle!" exclaimed Turok, his heart beating and breast heaving with violent emotions.

"It is she, sure as I'm a living man!" replied Prideaux. "That creature, like a spirit, is in every place. She's an angel, and blessed be the man who wins her heart!"

The young Iroquois made no reply, but stood and gazed upon her fair form as if he were indeed beholding an angel. The beautiful nymph stood bending over the noble officer as he lay upon the ground in the struggles of death.

"Are you fatally wounded, sir?" she inquired, in a voice full of sympathy and love, bending over his prostrate form, and wiping the big drops of perspiration from his manly brow.

"I'm a dying man," he faintly uttered. "Who are you, an angel come to minister to my wants in this, my last extremity?"

"I'm Lucelle, the daughter of an old hunter who lives but a short distance from the fort," she replied, while a tear dropped from her dark eye and fell on his noble face.

He felt the precious drop on his cheek, and oh! how he longed to live to reward this girl for that single tear.

"Oh! my God! The pains of death are upon me, and I've but a few moments in which to do deeds that a whole life would hardly be long enough to do them!" feebly said the dying colonel. "Mortal woman, or angel, whichever thou art, feel in my pockets, and take hence my watch and a purse of gold. Do so, while I have consciousness to know that they belong to a woman who shed a tear over me in my dying moments."

"Nay, sir. I would not take your gold for my tears," she replied, while other drops chased each other down her fair cheeks. "They spring from the soul whence gold cannot bring them. They flow freely, and ask not for reward."

"Take my watch and purse unless you wish to add another pang to those which are already wringing my heart with keenest anguish!" said the gallant Townshend, making an effort to reach his pockets for the articles which he was so anxious to give her, but his strength was too feeble and his effort failed. "Take them, fair nymph, for I've not strength to reach them. Oh! God! how the pains torture this poor frame. But they will soon pass away, and I shall be free!"

Lucelle, with streaming eyes and trembling hand, took from his pocket, his gold watch and silver purse. At this moment Turok came up to witness the sad scene.

"He's dying, and a brave officer he was too," said Turok.

"There, you've got them in your own fair hands, and keep them in remembrance of me," faintly said the dying Townshend. "I die in the cause of my country. Take me to your father's lodge, and let my body be decently buried. Ah! another is here, (opening his eyes upon the young Indian). You, whoever you are, friend or foe, will be a witness that this fair maid did not steal the watch and gold from a dying man, I gave them to her, and would to God they were a thousand times more valuable!"

"I'm no enemy to the dying," replied Turok, gazing with deep emotion upon the haggard countenance of the dying officer. Lucelle needs no witness, for no one would believe that she would steal from the living or the dead."

The gallant young officer now by a great effort partially raised himself upon one elbow, cast one anxious look upon Lucelle, fell heavily back upon the ground and expired.

"He's dead!" exclaimed Lucelle, bending over the corpse, and sobbing as if her heart would burst with grief and sorrow at the spectacle before her. His dying request shall be obeyed. Get some help and let us carry his body to my father's."

"It shall be done as you wish," said Turok. "Although he was our foe when living, now he's dead he can be the enemy of none. The grave to which he must soon be carried, covers all alike, whether friend or foe, bond or free, high or low, Indian or white man, all are on a level there, and all passions are hushed and still."

The body of the gallant Townshend in accordance with his dying request, was carried to the lodge of the old hunter. Lucelle selected a spot on the margin of the brook just above her mother's grave. Young Turok excavated the earth from the hill side, and the body of the British officer was deposited in the grave which the noble Iroquois dug with his own hands. Lucelle carried from the shore of the lake a flat piece of lime-stone and placed it over the remains of the gallant Townshend to mark the spot where he was buried.

When Townshend was shot and fell, his men whom he had led so boldly up to the fort, thinking he was instantly killed, fled from the scene of danger, and hurried with the sad tidings to General Amherst. They did not reach the encampment until after nightfall. The tidings were painful in the extreme to the gallant general, for he loved young Townshend, and placed great confidence in his judgment and military tact. The soldiers were busily engaged in preparing for the attack upon the fort early in the morning.

"Dead!" exclaimed General Amherst.—"The noble Townshend shot by the French rascals! Sad tidings indeed."

"Yes, we left him dead, and fled with the news," replied one of the soldiers.

"Where were you when he fell?" inquired Amherst. "Was it a musket ball which did the work of death?"

"We were before the breastworks of the fort, beyond the reach of their longest guns as we supposed," replied the soldier. "But a cannon ball reached our noble commander, and laid him low. A single gun only was fired."

"His death shall be revenged ere another sun sinks in the west," said the brave Amherst. "See to it that your guns, fellow soldiers, are clean and in good order. We'll give the French dogs such a breakfast as they cannot easily digest. We may mourn the loss of the noble-hearted and gallant Townshend, but his death must be revenged, else I die before the wall of that old fort. Last year the gallant Lord Howe fell there. Let us be prepared for the morrow. Victory must be ours."

True as General Amherst said, the gallant Howe did fall there, not twenty paces from the spot where the noble and accomplished Townshend received his death wound. All was now excitement in the ranks of the British army, and every necessary arrangement was made for the coming day.

CHAPTER VIII.

ALL was bustle, confusion, and excitement at the fort after Colonel Townshend was killed, and his reconnoitring company had retreated. Some of the French officers were encouraged to hold on and defend the fort, while others, and a large majority too, were for abandoning their position, setting fire to their works, and leaving for Crown Point. There were many discussions upon the point, and some of them were rather passionate and angry. Prideaux told them that it would be a vain task to attempt to defend the garrison long against such a force as the British were about to bring against it. Although he had directed the gun that had cut down the flower of the British army, yet he had too much knowledge of the movements and force of the enemy to be encouraged by this circumstance. The young Iroquois, too, was decidedly in favour of the French abandoning the fort, and perfectly united in opinion with Prideaux. He said the death of the gallant Townshend, instead of diminishing the ardour of the British, would urge them on with more fury and zeal,

After much deliberation upon the question, the officers and soldiers of the fort agreed to abandon it and let the British take possession of it without let or hindrance. Taking everything with them they could carry, and setting fire to the remainder, they secretly left the fort in the night, and repaired to Crown Point. In their hurry and excitement, they left their heavy artillery and several boats, which they sunk in the lake. The French at this time were evidently dispirited and discouraged, and the British, on the other hand, were much elated and saw victory in all their movements.

The next morning the French abandoned the fort, Gen Amherst wth his army

No 7.

appeared before the smoking walls. Finding none to defend, he quietly took possession of the fort, and encamped within the French lines. This important acquisition was effected without much opposition or bloodshed; but the pleasure of it was greatly diminished by the fall of the beloved and accomplished Townshend. Amherst soon began to repair and enlarge the fortifications, and to prepare his batteaux and other vessels for an expedition against Crown Point. Scouring and ranging parties were immediately employed, hovering in the vicinity of Ticonderoga, and watching all the measures and motions of the enemy. In a few days information was brought to Amherst that the French had also abandoned Crown Point. The general immediately detached a body of rangers to take possession of the place. Early in the month of August, he embarked with an army, landed at Crown Point, and placed his troops within the enemy's works. Thus was easily effected the reduction of Ticonderoga and Crown Point—two places which had given security to the inroads of the enemy, and afforded an asylum to the scalping parties which for a long period had infested the frontiers of the whole country, and cost the British colonies immense sums of money, and the lives of thousands of her citizens.

No sooner was the conquest completed, than Amherst superintended the works, strengthened and enlarged the old ones, and began a new fort, determined that the enemy should never again obtain possession of a post which had been so dangerous and distressing to the British provinces. The French troops, after the evacuation of Crown Point, retired to the Isle Aux Maix at the north end of the lake, and there strengthened their position by the addition of several battalions, five piquets of regular troops, and a body of Canadians and marines, the whole being provided with a numerous artillery and every requisite of defence. General Amherst could not proceed down the lake till he had constructed a naval force superior to that of the French.

The French lieutenant, Delano, had recovered from the effects of the spasms he had suffered previous to the victory which the English were now enjoying, and began to swell around and assume his former pomposity; but in spite of all he could do, he was not able to shake off the stigma which was deeply branded upon his character, and he became the laughing stock of the whole British army. This of course naturally soured his temper and disposition, which were none too good before. Amherst was not afraid to let him have his liberty, for there was no danger of his seeking the French army. His cowardice was a sufficient guarantee against any occurrence of that kind. He had seen Lucelle but once since her interview with him in the woods, when she was *en route* with intelligence for the commander of the fort, of the movements of the British army. He was then treated quite coldly by her and her father also; but this treatment served only to arouse the spirit of revenge within his breast against the old hunter, and to urge him on to secure the daughter as well as the money he knew was in the lodge.— Both these he was determined to obtain if within his power. The thought of murdering the father had already entered his soul, and darkened his spirit. He feared the young Iroquois more than any one else, as he was occasionally hovering about in the vicinity, and occasionally visiting Lucelle, although much against the will of her father.

She had not yet, it is true, determined on taking the Indian for her husband, and still she knew she loved him more than she did or could any other person. But pride still held the ascendency over love; this, together with her father's influence, had as yet restrained her from accepting the proposals of the young Iroquois. He did not press his suit in the usual way adopted among lovers, by making violent protestations of love, and telling her his heart would break, and that he should pine away and die of grief if she did not marry him; but he did let her know by his acts of kindness that he loved her. She was fully sensible that such acts could not proceed from a heart that did not love, and love sincerely and truly too. They spoke to her more eloquently than any words, gifted in speech as he was, he could have uttered.

The idea of going to Paris still had charms for her, notwithstanding she had given up all hope of being accompanied by Lieutenant Delano. Her father still cherished the hope of seeing once more his native city. True, the bright visions which the very pompous lieutenant had created were faded away, but still the old and long cherished hope was left to keep his heart whole.

Not long after the French evacuated the fort at Ticonderoga, and the British had taken possession of it, Lucelle and her father were seated on a bluff which commanded a good view of the lake, conversing about this contemplated journey to Paris, and other matters. The air was calm, a gentle breeze fanning their cheeks and slightly rippling the smooth surface of the lake.

"These are beautiful scenes, father, and I should regret to leave them," she said, leaning her head on his shoulder, and brushing back the grey hairs from his wrinkled brow. "Don't you think I should sigh for this wild scenery, and this beautiful lake if I were in Paris, where I could see no brooks nor trees?"

"You would see so many beautiful things there you would forget that you had been brought up in this wild forest," he replied, smoothing her polished forehead, and looking into her dark eyes.

"But we shall not be here to listen to the gentle breezes as they sigh through the branches of these trees, nor hear the music of that brook," she replied "Would to Heaven we could carry the graves with us."

"Tell me, Lucelle, if there's nothing else you would carry with you?" he inquired.

"Oh, yes, father, the brook, the trees, and this beautiful lake," she answered.— "I would carry all with me, that my eyes might see them until death should place his seal upon them, and shut out the light of day."

"To be plain and frank with you, Lucelle, I would ask if the young Iroquois does not make you love these scenes more than you would if you had never seen him?" he inquired.

She hung her head in silence for a few moments, and then said,—

"Turok asked me how I should feel to leave my mother's grave? He said he would not leave his father's grave, for he should be unhappy if he did."

"The Indians think more of their ancestors' graves than the civilized white people," he replied. "Ah! Lucelle, Turok is a cunning, shrewd Indian. But few Indians of his age are so cunning as he is. I've never known one more so. He alluded to your mother's grave purposely to make you more reluctant to leave these scenes. There are many in Paris who would be attracted by your beauty, and seek your hand. Think of these things, Lucelle, before you give your hand to an Indian. You may have children, and how should you feel to be the mother of half Indian children!"

Lucelle's pride was alarmed; for her father knew exactly what string to play upon, and what chord of her heart to touch. She made no reply to his remarks, but her countenance told the struggle which pressed her heart. It was a struggle between pride and love—a contest which sometimes severely agitates the human soul. Had she been called upon at this moment, and compelled to give an answer, pride would have carried the day and gained the victory over love, aided and strengthened by parental influence as it was in her case.

"See! father, Turok is coming now across the lake!" she exclaimed, evincing more anxiety in her voice and countenance than the old man liked to see, or than she would have been willing to express, if she had had time for reflection before she spoke. But the impulse of her heart showed itself ere she was aware of it, or before she thought of what her father had been telling her.

Most gracefully did the young Iroquios paddle his birch canoe across the lake towards the place where they were sitting. It skipped over the water like a thing of life, while the owner sat straight as an arrow, motioning his arms, and dipping his paddle into the placid bosom of the lake in measured time. Lucelle thought she never saw him look more beautiful and interesting than at that moment. Oh, how she wished he was not an Indian! But she would not have his face, form, color of skin, expression of countenance, or a single feature changed, and yet she wished the white man's blood ran in his veins.   He was an Indian, and O, how deep was her regret !   She would change his blood, but not a hair of his head.

Soon he ran his canoe into the brook alongside of Lucelle's, and ascended the teps to the spot where she and her father were seated.   Even the old hunter h m-self could not help greeting the young Indian cordially, he appeared so manly graceful and dignified, but yet he was determined his daughter should never wed one of the Iroquois tribe.

"Have you seen Delano within a few days," [said Turok.

" But once, and I think he will not show his head this way again very   on," she replied.

"I'm not so sure of that," said Turok, shaking his head and looking very serious.

" What mean you by these anxious looks?" inquired Lucelle.

" Did Delano inquire whether you had any money or not ?" asked Turok, ad-dressing the old man.

" We did have some conversation about money awhile ago," he replied.   " But Delano appeared to be indifferent at the time."

" Did you tell him how much you had ?" asked Turok.

" I believe I did," replied the old man.

" Yes you did," said Lucelle anxiously. " It was when you and he were talking about going to Paris."

" Then beware of that man, and always be prepared for the worst, for although he is a coward, he is desperate, and may attempt to do deeds even beyond himself. Disappointed in love, laughed at by the British army, and stung with the spirit of revenge, he may even attempt to commit murder, and steal your money and your daughter."

" He's too much of a coward for that, but nevertheless, I will heed your admonitions, for I know they spring from worthy motives," replied the old man.

" Enough !" said Turok.   " I must leave you for the present."

" Where do you propose to go now ?" inquired Lucelle, in the voice of kindness and solicitude.

" To the place where I was born—to the spot were my father was buried.   It has been some days since I stood over his grave.   I feel as if there was something lacking when I have been long absent from that sacred spot," said Turok, bound-ing away into the woods, and leaving them to wonder at his sudden flight.

CHAPTER IX.

Two days had passed since Lucelle saw the young Indian.   On the third day ; just at nightfall, she was sitting at the door of the lodge, anxiously waiting for her father's return.   He went out that afternoon, but did not return quite so soon as she expected him.   While she was thus waiting, she saw her father ap-proach.   When he had reached within a few paces of the door where she was, a loud report of a gun fell upon her ears, and at that moment her father leaped rnom the ground and fell dead at her feet.   A bullet had pierced his heart.   She e ntly arose and bent over the prostrate form of her father ; but his lips were red up, and his eyes were glazed.   Death had placed his seal upon his aged w.   While she was in this attitude, Delano came out of a thicket of bushes r by and approached her, unobserved. He came up close behind her, and ore she was aware of his presence, said,—

" Lucelle, dear Lucelle, it was I who shot your father, and all for the love I have for you. Now you must be mine. We will go home, for you shall live no more in these forests. There's money enough in the lodge, and we can live happy together."

" Never vile wretch !" she replied. " Death were indeed a blessing compared with such a fate ! Out of my sight, monster ! I cannot longer endure thy preence ! Begone foul murderer !"

" Call me not by such hard names, or I here swear you shall lies as low as your father," he answered, stepping to seize her by the arms.

At this moment the young Iroquois rushed to the scene of danger, and seized Delano by the shoulder, exclaiming,—

" Wretch ! I'm too late to save the father from your cowardly shot, but the daughter shall be shielded from your polluting touch.'

And the young Indian hurled the dastardly coward to the ground as if he had been a child in his powerful grasp.

" Mercy ! I pray thee !" exclaimed the trembling scoundrel, " Oh, spare me ! and I will never again be seen in these forests. Oh, do spare my life, and I will leave this place for ever."

" Never !" replied Turok, raising his tomahawk. " Die, thou monster for thou art not safe to run at large."

And he buried his tomahawk in his forehead quite up to the eye. One groan, and all was over. The French officer was a corpse at his feet.

" There ! the fatal deed is done," continued Turok. " He was so vile while he lived that he does not deserve a burial now he's dead. I will throw the dead body from yonder bluff into the lake, and let what fish that will, feed on the loathsome carcase."

" Oh ! my God," exclaimed Lucelle. " Forgive me for wishing that my deliverer was not an Indian. And thou, Turok, forgive my thought. I rejoice that thou art what thou art : for I would not have thee changed."

And she threw her arms about his neck, and for the first time in her life she kissed him. He felt the pressure of her warm lips on his cheeks, and a thrill of joy passed through his heart. Never before was the young Iroquois so happy as at this moment. Years of joy seemed to be compressed into a single moment, and he thanked the Great Spirit that he had lived to witness such an hour.

At length Turok exclaimed, gazing upon the dead bodies before him,

" Your father's body must be buried beside your mother's, but Delano's doe not deserve a burial."

The fair maid stood in silence for a few moments, as if she were wrapped in deep reflection.

" Nay, Turok, although Delano was a graceless villain while he lived, yet, nwel he's dead, let us bury our resentments with his body. He, too, belonged to the human family. However much we might have despised his wicked soul, let us now that soul has gone to its creator, decently bury the body which it once animated. Let us not visit the iniquities of his soul upon his lifeless body. His form is the same as ours, and the idea of throwing it into the lake, to be devoured by the fishes, or other creatures which inhabit the water, is revolting to the feelings of my heart. No, no, Turok, although he has murdered my father, and perhaps would have shed my blood, if I had not yielded to his wishes, yet I will not seek revenge upon the dead."

The young Indian stood and gazed, first on one lifeless form and then on the other. He did not at first feel the force of Lucelle's reasoning. Bright and talented as he was, he had some of the Indian's notions. He had always such a hate against Delano while he lived, that he could not have any regard for his body now that he was dead. To give it a decent burial was more than he thought justice required, according to his ideas of justice. The remarks of Lucelle set him to hinking.

" My first impulse was to throw his body into the lake," he said. " But why should I harbour the spirit of revenge against a lifeless form, which has not power

to do good or hurt.   You may be right, and your wishes shall be gratified.   I will
bury the body, but not near where your father is buried.   I will carry it beyond
the brook, and deposit it in some place where we may not see the grave."

"Do so, Turok, and I shall feel better satisfied than if you threw it into the
lake as you would the carcase of a dog," she answered. " It is human, and I would
not willingly see it become a prey to the wild creatures of the forest, or the fishes
of the lake,"

Turok now took the body of Lucelle's father, and carefully laid it out on a bench
in the lodge.   He then carried the body of Delano across the brook, and buried it
with the clothes on in a bye place.   After he had performed this service over
the last remains of the French lieutenant, he dug the grave for the body of the
old hunter beside that of his wife, and decently interred it.   Lucelle found a stone
upon the shores of the lake, and with her own hands placed it at the head of the
grave.   It was really an interesting, but melancholy spectacle, to see these lovers
performing the last sad rites over the earthly remains of a departed friend.   But
no funeral in town or city was ever conducted with more solemn feeling and purer
emotions than this was.   Long did the mourners linger over the grave after it was
filled with earth, and many a tear was shed upon that sacred spot.

Turok after the death of Lucelle's father never left her, and it is hardly needful
to add that in the course of a few months they were married.   A happier couple
was not to be found in those regions.   They lived in the same lodge in which
Lucelle's father resided ever since her birth.   Their union was blessed with several
beautiful children.   When they were married they assumed the name of her father,
and by that they were ever afterwards known and called.   Even at the present
day there are living in Canada some of the grandchildren of this worthy couple;
but few traces of the Indian blood are left by which they can be distinguished.
That the crossing of the breed improves the stock, was amply verified in the case
of Turok and Lucelle, for their children and children's children were among the
most enterprising and talented of the age.

But we must bring our historical narrative to a close.   The conquest of Canada
was completed in September of the year 1760.   The war continued six years, and
six battles were fought during the struggle, the fortune of which was equally
divided.   The first of these was fought at the meadows, near fort Du Quesne, in
which Braddock was slain and the French were successful.   The next contest
took place at Lake George, where Duskau was defeated, and taken prisoner.
The third was at Ticonderoga, in which Abercrombie was defeated, and Montcalm
gained the victory.   The fourth was at Niagara, where the French were com-
pletely overcome.   In the fifth, which was fought on the plains of Abram,
Wolfe and Montcalm both fell, two of the greatest, most accomplished, and bravest
generals that ever appeared in America.   But the British gained the victory.   The
sixth was at Sillery.   In this battle Murray was defeated, and M. de Livy was
victorious.   The grand contest for which the war was begun, was now decided.

The British nation and colonies, for more than seventy years had been endea-
vouring to accomplish this work, but without success.   A large country was now
added to the British dominions, and an end put to the depredations and ravages
of the Indian tribes : and the future prospects of the colonies bore the aspect of
tranquillity, prosperity, rapid increase and improvement.   All these hopes seemed
to be realized by the treaty of peace signed at Paris three years afterwards.   By
this treaty the King of France ceded and granted to the British king in full right,
the whole country of Canada with all its dependencies.

THE END.

www.ingramcontent.com/pod-product-compliance
Lightning Source LLC
Chambersburg PA
CBHW081215170626
46811CB00010B/3299